SPY THRILLER

THE SLEEPER SERIES

MONEY CAN'T LIE

By Anna Schlegel

BOOK ONE

Translation from Russian

Schlegel Press Association

Money Can't Lie by Anna Schlegel
Book One of The Sleeper Series

Published by Schlegel Press Association
Friedrichstr. 123
Berlin, Germany 10117

ISBN: 9780998185330

First Edition: October 2016

Translated by Alla Koshechkina
Cover photography by Alamy & Maxim Shirkov /Shutterstock

"...The Sleeper Series is a modern, fast-paced spin on British Intelligence operations that offers an entirely different perspective on why intelligence people become defectors."
- *MSNBC*

"...spy novel, promising to unravel the tangled web of a strange couple caught in the middle of an espionage game of British intelligence."
- *The Huffington Post*

"...a thriller that begins with a couple's discussion about intelligence processes and evolves to a cat-and-mouse game played out across the streets of Europe."
- *Midwest Book Review*

Also By Anna Schlegel

THE SLEEPER SERIES

WHO SPREADS FOR WHOM
Book Two of The Sleeper Series
The British intelligence cannot compromise its integrity, it will adhere to its principles like in the old times of rock 'n' roll. And it's damn good to look at it working... but then it's scary to see it work against you.

THE GODS SMILE ON THE BASTARDS
Book Three of The Sleeper Series
Once you are able to see the intelligence's handwriting, you may see the words of failure inscribed in the same handwriting, telling of a failure they are yet unaware of.

ONLY ONE REALITY THAT KILLS
Book Four of The Sleeper Series
It happens to everyone without exception. It will inevitably happen to you unless you live under the wing of the legend.

LIE MAKES ME LIVE
Book Five of The Sleeper Series
This game of the intelligence, we were either to see through it, or die.
Coming soon

Also By Anna Schlegel

THE DEAD BANK DIARY SERIES

THE DEAD BANK DIARY
Book One of The Dead Bank Diary Series
The rats living on the refuse of the bank's backyard stay full at all time.

FOR THOSE IN THE SHADE
Book Two of The Dead Bank Diary Series
You may live your whole life without getting to know who you are, and sometimes this is for the better.

THE PRINTS ON THE SNOWS OF YESTERYEAR
Book Three of The Dead Bank Diary Series
The best one to rob the bank is the banker himself.

SOME DAY I'LL HIT A BANK
Book Four of The Dead Bank Diary Series
The bomb lives to its internal time.

THE FROZEN DEBT
Book Five of The Dead Bank Diary Series
When totally nude have a look, maybe you still have the shoulder loops.

CONTENTS

AUTHOR'S NOTE

What do the defectors really want? Why do these people betray their country and friends? Why are some of those defectors lucky, while some others are not? Why don't they ever have any regrets?

What are their true motives? Is it about money? No. Do they do it for fear? No. Do they sometimes wish to build their careers in this alternative way? No. Are they seeking fame? No. Have they been brainwashed? No. Can they be naive idealists? No.

Whatever answers you may think of, all of them would be probably wrong.

Are they betrayers? Yes, they are. Are they doing the right thing? Yes, they are. Do they find in this treachery what they must have been looking for? They sometimes do. How can they live with this? They are perfectly in tune with their own selves.

What are their goals? Now you will have the answer. It is worth knowing. This answer will surely change the way you see the world. This will be the answer from the legend.

Should there be three pieces of crap, this is of the British Intelligence classic

MONEY CAN'T LIE

He was not worth a straw to Intelligence; he was a mere sleeper, just a small coin. One day he felt that, behind his back, there was someone else; a big shot of such high value that they could not afford to lose him. Who could that be - a recent defector? He had no idea.

He could only sense a trace of him, barely there; just a nip. They were seeking to ward off the trail, and not just by drawing it aside. Now it appeared to lead straight to him. Every little thing pointed to him.

The trace would be lifeless, classically beautiful, and, as such, stone-dead.

ABOUT THE SLEEPER SERIES

Each of the secret services has its own handwriting, faint and hardly perceptible. This handwriting is their custom. It does not change for years, and one can read it through. This handwriting can lead an agent to failure. This is what these books are written about, if anything.

These books also tell of the legend that keeps recruiting people across time and distance; of something that is stronger than life. This legend is an eternal truth, refilled with the living blood of every new recruiter who would choose the way of the legend. These books are about the legendary Kim Philby.

These books contain neither facts of Kim Philby's life nor any historical events. This is all about the modern-day, and is pure fiction.

I'm giving an answer to the question: Why should the legend of Philby be everlasting? Why is this legend of Philby such a deadly, pulling force? How do the people survive under the wing of his legend?

There is little said about it, yet this is the main point.

They become traitors long before they step across the threshold of the spy directorate. They step across expressly to turn into traitors one fine day. That is the way they see their careers. They wish to re-act that life of the icon. The legend of Kim Philby makes them traitors from the moment they open that book of his or read about him. This legend keeps recruiting people without money or contracts. The reality is forceless against it. The legend keeps dictating its own logic. It may come along imperceptibly. Once the book of the legend is read through and half-forgotten, it sprouts deep inside and lives to its own time, so one day it will casually remind of its existence, in an implicit way, and push its follower to make the decision which he must have prepared for long ago, when an occasion was in short supply.

Most paradoxically, such agents appear to be more mature, and do not really care much about public recognition, awards, money, appreciation, and all those matters connected with a regular, rewarding career. They do not really fall for the uniform and regalia. Surely, the traitors get incomparably better money, but it was not always this way, and would never be the main point. These people rate themselves so highly that money does not measure that value. They are, essentially, free.

For such people, there is no borderline where they become traitors; they must have since long slipped across by taking no notice. These people are usually well-educated and highbrow, and, as such, intelligently cruel and deeply calculating.

They are idealists. The philosophy of theirs makes blood turn to ice. This is how the legend of Kim Philby works. And it's a damn good British job.

CHAPTER ONE

SILENT PARTNER

Moscow-Berlin, January 2011

Victor and I were waiting for Vlad in an empty ramshackle house in the suburbs of Berlin. There were a lot of similar houses for sale in the area. They were all half-empty or abandoned. Along the sidewalks there were grey trees with their crowns cut as if they were left dying there, growing old along with those houses around them. There was no sun. The sky seemed low under the gray mist and snow. Snowflakes were falling thick and heavy and weren't melting, but were stuck to the windowsills and tiny balconies hanging onto the walls like wasps' nests, settling onto the cords and poplar branches in the backyard which, from afar, resembled a scruffy wool clew. The black, dusty, curtainless windows drew the eye, their glass lit with the reflection of the snow. They looked totally blank.

The apartment echoed with the void behind its every wall, and it smelled of stale humid air, autumn bitterness, and empty house.

Dressed in a T-shirt and jeans and aproned in an old flannel blue-checked shirt, Victor started grilling sausages. The fireplace here was made of an angled, ceiling-high white tile stove that bumped up against the stucco's decorative border, incoherent with time, with the spring's damp patches soaked like a rum sponge cake. Soon the apartment filled with the smoke and odors of fat sizzling on coal, and the place warmed up. We drank some vodka, and it felt somewhat warmer.

"I can't recognize Berlin." Victor put aside his fork and sat back, gazing unseeingly out the window. "The streets look different, the people seem alien... Even the taste of bratwurst and bread has changed."

"Who is Vlad?" I asked him.

"Vlad Holt is a friend of mine. His true name is not Vlad. The partners to the deal are the only people to know him as Vlad Holt. The name Vlad Holt does not belong to anyone, really; it is used for the deal. This name is given through the deal to the person holding the arrangement under control, and then it may be passed on to another person. Should something happen to Vlad, I'll have to be Vlad Holt. All I have to do is make myself another passport. This is the way we orchestrated it, many years ago."

"And what about this being not his real name...?"

"The name is valid. Vlad made himself a passport over twenty years ago, when that was still possible."

Such passports could be made by intelligence people or fugitives when things got hot for them. They used to find a similar person in the passport archives of the police department, of someone who'd long ago left the country, and then just pasted in a different photo. Later on, the person would come back to tell the police he'd lost his passport and he would request a new one. Understandably, this scheme cost a lot and was unthinkable without proper links. One could still make a passport that way ages ago, at the time of the mess-up. Nowadays, one could still make a passport that way only in some of the former Soviet republics. The actual Vlad Holt had been living in America for a long time.

"And has this Vlad also got the whole setup, like housing, property, and credit cards?" I wondered.

"Yeah, and he owns a few companies, some bank accounts, and even has parking tickets."

"And has he got another name - his real name?"

"Yes, well, it's not quite a real name of his, but also comes with multiple credit cards, bank accounts, and traffic tickets ... never mind." Victor took a cigarette and pressed its crumpled filter with his tooth, then swept his eyes over the empty, snow-covered yard. "Vlad is younger than me; he's around fifty - yet I was thinking all this time, couldn't he get sick?"

"Has there been anyone else acting as Vlad, prior to him?"

"There used to be a friend of mine, when I started this operation. We actually needed all the parties to know just one single person who would be available on call at any time. Vlad comes to handle everything."

"And what happened to that Vlad?" But then, looking at Victor's face, which had grown sulky, I realized I'd better not ask.

"He perished," Victor said, gritting his teeth.

"Was that through this deal of yours?"

"No, he was accidentally disclosed. He was working for the intelligence. That also happens. But the people aware of this Vlad Holt's existence are just me and him and those partners of ours - nobody else, not even the bank, is informed about this. Vlad himself lives on his own passport."

"How come? Don't they know all of you, at the bank?"

"Many of us open accounts on behalf of a straw party, or use some middleman. Sometimes the chain of transactions is very long. Then there are also partners which you'd be better off knowing nothing about."

Hurst Bank handled all the major transactions and essentially lived on this deal only. It had taken Victor several years to make this business out of thin air, and he had plenty of personal contacts.

The partners to this arrangement, the majority of whom were high-ranking functionaries, military establishment members and diplomats, ministerial advisors, or company heads, preferred to have their dealings via close confidants, and the latter pulled their middlemen. It seemed the whole thing involved no one, really, but a number of intermediaries. And the chain worked as well-tuned clockwork that left no legible e-trace, like hawala.

As to how much commission and who of the partners and middlemen were getting paid, only Victor knew full well. Even the bank had nothing to say as to which of the partners or the founders of multiple offshore companies and nominal directors were behind those agents.

This was how I see it to this day. But then it turned out that Vlad was well informed of all the deal's participants. He was a shadow partner to this deal; the key to the scheme.

Vlad arrived by night. He was bright and fair-haired with gray temples and a high-bred face, as if he'd been parboiled in the sun. His dry, thin, and chapped skin seemed covered in dust, his sun-burnt eyebrows looked almost non-existent, his bloodless lips were almost lost on a white face peppered with hardly visible freckles, and he had a peaky bird-like nose. Under his narrow eyeglass lenses I could see his squinty eyes, so pale that they looked frozen under his eyelashes, which much resembled hoarfrost. One of his eyelids was somewhat lopsided, so it gave him a deadly, condescending look. He was damn sexy and he knew it. He seemed to trash people just passing by with a single glance. He looked rather stooped in his stretched wool jacket over broad shoulders, but then, one could sense there was still a lot of power in those shoulders. Taking a glance at him, I thought Victor should not worry; he was probably just tired.

They gave each other a hug. Vlad had a gulp of vodka as if just tasting it and pressed his lips, then settled at the table and squared his elbows, holding a cigarette in front of his face between closed fingertips. Victor clicked his lighter, covering his face with a palm, and looked at him expectantly.

"We've lost the bank," Vlad uttered, and fell silent.

"Is there anything else?" Victor asked him.

"Yes." Vlad shifted his gaze, ruminating. "I felt they've tracked me down. I could sense surveillance, but chose not to check it out. This feeling is enough for me. Oh gosh, it's been so long... It's like reliving your first love. I thought my heart might break. I've got to lie low now. I do not like to leave you at this time, but... I'm sorry, Victor, you'll have to be Vlad now."

CHAPTER TWO

RATS IN THE BANK

REFUSE

Victor was born in West Berlin. Looking at him, I would never think he had been a respectable banker for a good half of his life.

"I don't get it, Victor," I uttered, at a loss. "You've got nothing German in you... nothing at all. I would never think..."

"You are not so observant. Instead of *Thank you*, I'm accustomed to handing cash. That saves me a lot of useless trouble," Victor replied.

He was a robust, sated boar, if not for his sulky, tense face showing through his bristled beard. He had sunken, pale eyes surrounded by dark circles under his black eyebrows, with deep wrinkles crosscutting his forehead and cheek dimples. His broken, somewhat crumpled lips never smiled. I'd seen him that rigid and tense only once before, a while back, here in Berlin. He always wore the same suit, worth at least a thousand dollars but worn-out to one cent, and a coat fully impregnated with a cheap cigarette smell.

He used to live here with his father, working in a bank. His life was just like that of others till one day his father told him he wanted to have a rest, and left and never came back. Victor gradually replaced him and became the same kind of middleman, selling military information. Then he left for South Africa for two years and later returned to his banking affairs. He'd also spent two years in Moscow. Then he was back, and nothing had really changed much. Victor was expected to eventually take a considerably high position with the bank.

But when Victor brought to his bank the bargain of Congo foreign debt discharge, essentially made of his personal contacts and his father's links, he instantly took a seat on the bank board and became way too visible. They did not want him that way. So Victor was accused of spying for the Russians. There was no arrest, and neither searches nor evidence nor any noise whatsoever followed. The bank management just asked him to go.

Victor had been sold out for the sake of another agent, who remained in the shade and continued to move up a pace on the career ladder. That agent turned out to be his own wife.

So Victor had to go and leave behind his post in the bank, his business, his wife, and his two children from his first two marriages - all of his past life. He was free to live any place in the world except for Berlin. Victor opted for Moscow. Why so? Could he really have no grudge over the fact that he'd been burnt by the same intelligence he'd been working for? I often asked myself this question. Anyway, how could Victor live in Moscow? And why? Victor said that at some point his father had left for Argentina, had a house and a garden there, and his grandchildren, Victor's children, came to visit him there. So why was Victor staying in Moscow at all? I only understood the reason why some years back, when I was here with him in Berlin.

Victor had invisibly stayed in that deal since Hurst Bank's CEO, an old friend of his, could very well see the deal would not be workable without Victor. While living in Moscow, Victor was able to find out from where they should expect another punch against their deal.

At its core, the deal itself was initially Russian, as this was about the remission of Congo government debt to Russia. Hurst Bank in Germany used to buy out the bills from Russia in tranches. Victor's company would sell those bills to oil companies that paid in the same bills for their oil field development licenses. Then, after the oil sale, the money settled the accounts of all those parties. Since the bills were bought out prior to their due date, the government used to give them a discount.

At the market's crash, many Russian banks became bankrupt and the deal went on without their participation. But then, once fallen out of the deal, the Russian side still wanted to take part. This is why, one fine day, Hurst Bank found itself on the verge of a takeover. Victor was sure the Russian intelligence was behind it; this was way too obvious.

That time, Victor and I went to Berlin for a couple of days. The deal was restored and the Russian trace disappeared. But that was not yet the end of the whole story. This deal was too big a piece of cake.

Before meeting Victor, I never thought that kind of deal was at all possible. It was made of thin air; of noncommittal talks and handshakes. The deal consisted of intermediaries and representatives of the same. Victor would tell me of this deal, but it seemed to me that I was daydreaming. It was just like entering a mirror-world; my own imaginary world where I wanted so much to stay.

I had lived a long time in that world of ghostly millions and had no wish to get back to the real world. I wanted to stay in those times of the national default. This default had always been there with me. What to do? We seem unable to push away the times when we were happy; aren't we set there for good? They name my generation the "children of default". True, I still remained a child spoiled by an enormous amount of silly-money that used to easily come into my hands and just as easily leaked away between my fingers. I had the same kind of propensity for money that alcohol addicts have.

I could not put up with the fact that this time was long gone. I could still remember the smell of money hanging over my city, thick like a petrol haze in the heat above the highway. I was not ready to accept that I had been infected by those ghostly millions. They were long gone with the wind, somewhere far off, and surely had settled in the right place, in the narrow paved streets where the bank plate on the door is about the size of my palm. Later on I stopped reproaching myself for being a total failure. One day I felt inexplicable freedom from the fact that I was no longer dependant on anything, really. I could get along without money, on doles alone. It seemed I was able to put up with everything and wear the same gray raincoat and worn-out shoes for years. I had a forgettable white, sharp-looking face and a keen hungry look. I lived as a rat and I felt myself being a rat, and I rather liked it.

I learned to live in that expectation because I knew I had everything I needed to get my share of the cake. I aimed to raid some failing bank, which was not so difficult: at that time many people lived by raiding. Furthermore, quite recently there had burst out a banking crisis and one-third of all banks had become bankrupt in a single stroke. They kept falling like autumn leaves taken off trees by the wind.

In the beginning I was surrounded by a lot of people who'd lost their jobs and former links. They had to turn into off-board middlemen selling and purchasing all the waste spit up by the stock market, which was mostly about bankrupt banks and companies debts. However, as the years passed, things somewhat settled down and there were fewer and fewer of those middlemen; especially those who wished to make a fortune overnight by playing middleman for a megabuck deal. Over the course of time those links of mine, among which there were many worthless whitebeards, lost themselves into drinking and sank into oblivion. And if there still remained some, they were all hiding in their private apartments, as invisible as rotting windfall in the fresh grass.

Now Victor had turned up, thinking he'd bring his deal payments to Moscow.

This deal was already in Moscow like a sketch: somewhat ethereal, but should we have a bank of our own, it could get filled with real money that would become its blood. We were pressed for time. But then, how could we capture a bank with our bare hands? It did not work out, and the payments were still processed through Hurst Bank.

Sometimes I wondered what would have happened to my life if I had not met Victor?

"What's up with the bank?" Victor inquired.

"It's a lot worse, actually," Vlad uttered, blowing his cigarette smoke towards the half-open window. "I've learned that the bank set aside five million dollars for the settlement of that matter regarding suspicious transactions and money laundering. Since the sum is clear, the bank appears well informed of what transfers took place offshore and for which clients they are going to pay this penalty. That means the bank has come to terms with the tax office and the public prosecutor. That's it. The bank is as good as lost."

"Shit," Victor cursed. "Is that really so?"

"I was told the trashcans have been recently searched by some not quite dog-poor people. Yes, this is true. We should freeze the deal and start looking for another bank. I called you once I heard about it. And then, there is also a tail."

Vlad said he could sense that glance on his back, and he quickened his pace. He had a feeling there was another onlooker waiting for him around the corner. Vlad could not see him but he could almost feel his breath and anticipatory tension. Vlad swerved to pass through the market and then kept walking for a quite a while through the public garden where he could see every passer-by and check them out.

He decided not to go back home, spent three days in a motel, and when going out, passed every time through the same public garden; but he still could not shake off the feeling that there was a tail. Before going upstairs to this apartment of ours, he'd wandered around the neighborhood for about half an hour.

"Vlad, let us not take any risks; you should fly the coop now. Can you go back to Canada?" Victor asked.

"Let us first puzzle this out. I won't go anywhere unless we understand if this is truly so. I don't get it. Maybe I was just seeing things that weren't there? I felt so strange, as if I was taken back twenty years and not a damn thing had changed. A tail! Can those bastards ever change their habits? So that you understand, rock 'n 'roll is still alive." Vlad wanted to smile, but he could not.

"I had the same story when I'd just moved to Moscow, walking about the city, looking up an office and a flat, and those surveillance guys followed me. Can you imagine: Moscow was starving with no jobs whatsoever and everybody scattered around some private firms, but then, no fucking shit, they still follow you as if it were the holy seventies?" Victor smiled and bared his tooth, pressing a cigarette.

After a drink, Vlad was somewhat defrosted, and inspecting him with a dramatically pejorative tone, Victor uttered:

"Holy shit, Vlad, you look as crumpled as ever. Do you remember us the first time? You came to my company some ten years ago wearing the same old pants..."

"What, have you got anything against my pants?" Vlad snapped back at him good-naturedly.

"Well no, nothing; they just look kind of crumpled, there..." Victor remarked.

"And maybe you don't like this mug of mine, do you? Or is it also crumpled?" Vlad teased him.

"No, nothing; it's just sort of unshaven..."

"Lay off, or I'll set your mind at rest with a facer." Vlad finally gave a grin.

"Vlad, I was just checking to see if it's truly you, or somebody else," Victor retracted.

"That was a high risk. Fine, dash it, I'll have a good sleep and bash your face tomorrow so that you remember me," Vlad grumbled, getting up.

"Vlad, tell me, what else is there?" Victor inquired, running his eyes over Vlad's face.

"I had two calls over the last week. Nothing special, but … One is an interpreter from the US embassy and he probably wants an advance payment. And another one is a consulting company owner, an ex-intelligence agent who lost contact with his middleman." Vlad named the people and added, growing sulky, "Something's wrong there. I've got a sinking feeling."

CHAPTER THREE

BIRD OF PASSAGE

Vlad put his feet up for a while, hardly started to doze, woke up again, drank another vodka, and couched.

Victor and I were sitting in the kitchen in silence, smoking at the window. The darkness of the night overtook the entire inner yard. A couple of lanterns were shining through the bare branches of the high poplars, and they seemed so close that I could stretch my arm out and touch them. Everything looked flat, like a black-and-white glossy photo. The steam of my smoky breath was hanging in white plumes in front of my face and remained undissolved as if I were breathing out against the wall. Somewhere in

31

the distance car wheels harshly crunched on the snow, and the echo spread that crunch with a glass-like shriek. It was growing cold.

"Is Vlad in danger?" I wondered, looking into Victor's sulky face.

"I don't know. The worst thing is that someone's trying to grab this deal, and this someone decided he'd found a clue - that is Vlad - so he wants to press him or knock him out, thinking the chain will then disintegrate."

"Does that mean someone who got to know Vlad is familiar with all participants to the deal, so they started haunting him?"

"Maybe. Or then, maybe something from his past has come to the surface... Who could need him now that he's been long forgotten?"

"And what has Vlad gotten into?" I wondered, starting to guess.

"He's a bird of passage. He's been on the sidelines for a long time, over twenty years now. Nobody needs him anymore. No one's been paying him attention for a long time. For all these years, nobody's ever made contact with him; and if they ever did, it would mean an explicit trap. If something like that happened, Vlad would call the police straight away."

"Victor, could any of those clients get arrested?"

"No. There is nothing illicit in these transactions. The point at issue could be the client himself, as he may have problems with the law in some other place."

"So what are you thinking of doing?" I wondered.

"I don't know. I'll have a drink first. Would you like some vodka?" Victor took out a chilled bottle from the freezer, poured us some, and then, casting a glance towards the half-open door where Vlad was in restless sleep, he said, "I'll tie up the deal till they get off the bank, or just find another bank. I'll have to warn everyone out there. And then let's see what is behind those two calls Vlad received just recently."

"Could there be something wrong with those calls?" I questioned him, moistening my throat with the burning vodka's bitterness.

"If someone seeks to grab the deal and thinks that by knocking out Vlad, he could destroy the communication between the participants, then probably that appointment is to make sure Vlad actually exists; that is, to pin him down. Or then again, maybe he's already been traced, but they lost his trace and one of those calls is intended to bring Vlad into the open. I don't know," Victor said reflectively.

"And what about that other appointment? Is that for confirmation?"

"Not necessarily. If Vlad noticed that tail, this was probably a warning threat. They might wish him to notice the surveillance and understand that this is a threat. And such threats are often followed by a bargain offer. I guess the second call could be an invitation for the talks, or they might give some condition to Vlad. It would also be good to know what this intruder wants, or who this intruder is."

"Could they have Vlad arrested?"

"They have no reason to, but then there is a good point in seeing him, to make sure he truly exists."

"Will you go to these appointments? It's quite risky if you are left alone," I said.

"And who says I'm alone out there? Tomorrow, get your ass off early. Now you have to get some sleep, and I'll smoke some more here."

It seemed weird. Where should we go? I even had no idea why Victor had taken me along to Berlin this time. In the doorway, I turned.

"Victor, excuse me, one more question. It just came to my mind..." I didn't finish saying and I did not know how to ask *Could this Vlad have sold the deal to someone himself, along with all the participants, once they got him by the short and curlies?*

It's hard to live when you feel yourself to be a walking strongbox.

Victor understood without a word.

"No, it makes no sense." Victor brushed it off casually.

"Is there any backup?"

"Yes."

"And what is it? Something like a safety deposit box?"

"It's a cipher code; a two-key code that only two people know, and it cannot be decoded without Vlad. As you see, the list of people informed of all those partners is not so long - just Vlad and me."

"That means there are only two of you..."

"Oh my goodness, what are you thinking there, bunny?" Victor seemed to be reading the thoughts on my face.

I was probably looking at Victor with my eyes full of fear. He added that the list meant pretty much nothing, by itself. Vlad could hand it over and tell them about everyone and nothing would happen. The people on that list were friends of Victor, or those who owed him something. And one cannot just approach a diplomat and say, *Look, I heard you are making money on some bill's resale; let us strike a bargain and I'll start paying you...* All you'd hear would be, *Would you kindly fuck off.* And the whole thing would end there.

Vlad was simply running between those partners and middlemen who were all mistrustful, greedy, and bad-tempered. Naturally, some of them occasionally dropped out and some new people came in. They were all humans with their own weaknesses, and one could press them on every one. There was no point thinking the list was of much value in and of itself. This list would not be workable in other hands. To wrest this deal away would take as much time as creating it starting from scratch like Victor had.

"To collect all this incriminating evidence, one needs a lot of time. The tax investigator could not have done it in a blink, so someone's probably offered them information," I added.

Both this tail of Vlad's and the bank inspection could not be mere coincidences.

"I don't know. We've got to figure out why they were tracking Vlad. Could he have gotten it wrong? And then, who may need him, and why? I have to give it more thorough thought. I'll take another smoke here," Victor said, and kicked me aside with his glance.

"Victor, I've got another silly question ... How do all these people contact Vlad? Could they trace him with his cell?"

"No, people call his voicemail, and leave their phone number so he may call them back from a public pay phone. Or otherwise they contact him by means of a newspaper ad, or else... Will you go to bed now? I'll be damned, bunny!"

CHAPTER FOUR

VLAD

I'd hardly dropped asleep in my bed, which felt cold and fresh like a snow bank, when I woke up, hearing Vlad wash his hands again before using the toilet. Silently telling him where to go, I walked into the kitchen, lit my cigarette, and asked him in an irritated and sleepy voice, "Vlad, what the fuck? Why do you wash your hands before using the toilet?"

"I can't really hold my prick with my hands unwashed," he explained to me patiently.

He exited the toilet and washed his hands again. A plague on him.

"And why are you washing now?" I teased him.

"You won't understand," Vlad replied with disdain.

Having awakened again in the middle of the night, chilled with cold, I could see through the half-open door that Vlad was not sleeping. His crooked silhouette in the dim doorway was like a shadow; just a bit thicker, and his hardly-smoldering cigarette flashed for a moment, its rich fragrance filling the room. Vlad was sitting at his laptop with the screen light playing off his spectacles.

As I approached him, I could see he was tense, with a bit of sweat above his upper lip. In front of him sat a cup of lukewarm black coffee, a shot of vodka, and a full ashtray.

"What are you looking for?" I wondered, peeping at his screen.

"It must be stupid, but I still wonder whether all this shit could have happened because of me? Could I have stepped into some kind of crap out there? We now think someone from the outside is trying to grab the deal. It seems like it. But far more often, something like casual shit happens, so I like to make sure by checking through the archives, unorthodox resignations, and obituaries. I'm doing this kind of search now. We'd better start thrashing this out so I can leave with a light heart. I only *felt* that surveillance was there. I could have been mistaken. What if they don't need Vlad, but they want me - the kind of person I used to be twenty years ago? I think one day someone will come up to me and call out my name. Someone could remember and come on me... I seem haunted by the rock 'n roll." He screwed his face into a smile.

"It can't be so... there are a lot of shifty people involved in this deal who would sell their own grandmother for peanuts."

"Uh-huh... here it is; I've found one. A death notice - have a look." Vlad opened the ad page column. "Ben Meier, who called me in for an appointment, was reported missing three days ago. His wife placed this notice. He's an ex-operative. These people can't go missing. I guess he is no more. That is, this call came from a dead man. Yes, the voice was truly his, but..."

Victor came up, cat-like, to stand behind our backs. "That means this appointment is just to make sure you really exist. Me too - I've started thinking this way."

"I guess I've failed to find something. Why is she here?" Vlad gave a nod in my direction without looking at me.

"Couldn't you ask her yourself? Ann would own a bank, sooner or later. Sooner would be best," Victor replied unwillingly.

With the thought *What could I tell him myself?* I started getting what Victor was talking about.

"Victor, do you think Ilya would hand us his bank for this deal?" I wondered, and suddenly realized Victor had actually found this solution long time ago; maybe when I was only starting to date Ilya.

It seemed just yesterday that I had been in Moscow, and Victor asked me to drop in at his office and I'd thought, *Why?* I could count on my fingers how many times we'd encountered each other.

Late in the evening, I came up to an old, plain-looking, two-storied mansion with dusty windows behind a wrought iron gate, lost in the courtyards of the old city center, went up to the first floor, and passed through the corridor to Victor's office, where a streak of light shone under the door. Knocking on it with my knuckles, I pushed the door open and heard a snatch of Victor's voice:

"...what it means for the States to cast money against some security, well, I know it so very well, and if needed, I'd give you a proper instrument, but this money would not move. I've got enough securities approved by UBS bank alone, worth a billion dollars. If a certificate of deposit from UBS or Credit Suisse, or the top banks of France, Denmark, Belgium or the Netherlands is fine with your American friend, I'll send him one..."

"Do you mean, through the same bank?" a gentleman in an expensive business suit sitting with his back to me asked.

"Uh-huh, and then in this bank we put the subway in the pledge," Victor gave him a lop-sided careless smile, baring a yellow tooth that pressed his crumpled cigarette filter.

"Which one? The one in Moscow?" his stunned interlocutor wondered in a low voice.

"Erm, surely not that of New York, you simpleton," Victor snorted at him graciously and sat back looking at him through the puff of smoke coming out of his mouth.

That was a perfect joke. That was truly Victor. Once he noticed me, Victor gave his visitor a nod to show the conversation was over.

"Have a nice day," the man hastened to say goodbye quietly, like they do in unfamiliar environment, when in doubt about whether someone will pour you a vodka or beat your face. He grabbed his coat and slopped into the corridor.

"We got to go see Ilya, bunny," Victor told me, getting to his feet and taking a well-padded envelope with the documents from the table.

Ilya... What could have happened?

Ilya, the head of a minor bank in Moscow, was the person I was dating on weekends. I used to go to his country house. Sometimes, having decided we'd better leave these dates the way they were, those quiet evenings ended late at night on the verandah where we could sit and smoke together. We never changed it nor spoke about it.

Why? There were many reasons. Ilya had so many debts from which he wanted to get out from under. He was seventy-five and used to living alone. I had my crazy life: the kind of rat race that was hard to leave. To exit, I'd have to pay a lot of money, which I would never have. I would have to pay even more to enter Ilya's life. This entry appeared rather questionable, to me. It was unthinkable for me to enter that life of his as a beggar. I had to earn all this money on my own, or steal it. Naturally, we had never discussed this with Ilya, and he might have a different way of thinking - I had no idea - but the situation presented to me was only this. It looked as if I truly wanted to buy myself those evenings and nights with Ilya using this money, in that house where I was able to forget everything for two days. Ilya was worth it; Ilya was too dear to me.

I kept fighting for every cent, but it all flowed between my fingers. Essentially, I knew I still had a chance to catch a solid lump while other people knew nothing about it and left their piece to others. Worse, some of my contacts settled for a fixed wage and managed to sell themselves on the idea that the solid lump was just a fantasy, or that maybe it used to be real and now it was no more, and what remained available was just petty cash the size of sunflower seeds, only good enough to feed their family. How could they have changed so much? I did not want to know this. I was as good as dead to them, just like that past life of theirs. And they were right: who would need a not-so-young a woman with hungry eyes in permanent search of money to borrow, who had long time forgotten which world she was living in? I could not lead a different life; that other life would kill me.

We arrived at Ilya's country house in deep twilight. The backyard, covered in snow, was dark. Behind the apple garden, through the fine net of tree branches, the windows shone unusually close, nearby. Ilya was already there, back from the bank, waiting for me.

Under Victor's feet the frozen planks creaked and the cups on the table trembled with his heavy steps.

"Ilya!" I called him.

Ilya came out of the kitchen. He looked lean and high-brow with the round shoulders all tall people have and a face pale like snow; from which one instantly felt chilly. He seemed icy all over, with a cold glance from under his hollowing eyelids and a sharp glacial smile that seemed to cut people short and prevent them from approaching him.

I did not even try to get closer to Ilya any more than he wished it himself. Or, that only seemed so to me, earlier. Lately, I'd realized I used to unwillingly push him away from me, once quoting too high a price. Ilya did not try to bring the price down; rather, he accepted it, but then it only put him off even farther.

I could not imagine that one day Victor would get to know Ilya.

"Victor," he presented himself to Ilya.

45

When I first met Victor, he was about to arrange the takeover of Ilya's bank. At that time he requested I buy up the bank debts of some defense enterprise. Victor was buying up those debts one by one. The company director was a friend of Ilya's and he refused to sell his debt. In some way, this rescued Ilya. Ilya had the feeling I knew the person behind his bank takeover, and he seemed ready to disembowel me. I have no clue how I managed to avoid telling him everything, and probably for this reason alone I was now still there with him. And Victor retreated.

I could not imagine another life for myself without Ilya. Victor once told me that Ilya was willing to hold his enemy by the tits.

However, I had a different life, and Victor was always present there, without being noticed. It was running its course, quietly, like a clock mechanism ticking inside. I lived there, waiting for some falling bank to come my way so we could start the takeover. Then we would do it together again, with Victor.

But every time, it turned out I would not be able to survive without Ilya. Ilya pulled me out of all kinds of shit, but he could not really help me. He was in debt himself.

"Are you taking Ann with you?" Ilya nicked it, and offered his hand to Victor. "Let us skip the apologies and the punch fest. What's the matter?" Ilya invited him, with a gesture, to have some cognac.

"To your health," Victor nodded to Ilya, and drank it. "Vlad has called me to Berlin. He's a friend of mine who's keeping the deal under control. If Vlad is calling me, it means the deal is either crumbling or on the verge of failure. It's a bad sign."

"And what does it threaten?" Ilya inquired.

"In the worst case scenario, I'll have to replace him. But, you know, things are never too bad, so..." Victor did not say everything he wanted to say. He set an envelope full of documents before Ilya. "This is to be used in an emergency, in case I'm there no more and everything goes wrong. You could have a look at it, but you'd better not. It may still work out all right."

"I'll just have a look," Ilya said, taking a passport out of the envelope and opening it. "You mean it?" Ilya questioned, and his face froze as he unwillingly pulled away from Victor.

"I'm sorry to tell you that."

"You must be mad," Ilya said through his teeth, turning his back and putting the passport back.

His kiss was bitter and smelled of the cognac we drank, when we parted.

"Oh, you won't have to smooth-talk Ilya into this." Victor screwed up his face, making a wry mouth and watching my face fall, then turned to Vlad. "I'll call that wife of Meier's tomorrow; she must have phoned 'round all the hospitals by now. Or I'll make a call to his office. Was he still working in that consulting firm?" Victor wondered, and Vlad confirmed with a nod. "At least we know this call is probably to just have a look at you, good-looking. Where, exactly, has this Meier made an appointment?"

"Right here, close by, in the park, tomorrow morning."

CHAPTER FIVE

BURNT-OUT

In the morning Victor made a call to the office where Ben Meier worked and they told him the man was expected to come in on Monday. There was still a chance he'd just left his wife or chosen to lie low. He might be deep in debt, and had just made this appointment because he wanted some money? You never know, things do happen. But he would surely come to this appointment with Vlad.

Victor and I exited the taxi about two blocks away from the meeting point. My face was instantly frozen, peppered with prickly, salt-like powdered snow. Victor turned up his coat collar, gathered his scarf around his neck up to his nose, and tilted his wool hat over his eyebrows.

It was a quiet, bare park, deserted the way it may be only in wintertime, its pathways covered in snow that had somewhat melted under the feet of the passers-by and then iced up. The snow was blinded my eyes with its piercing white so that my closed eyes could still sense its white dazzling trace. We separated and started to detour into the park, circling. After one circle, I went back into the street, bought myself a hamburger and coffee, and then looked at the windows of the buildings facing the park. Nothing unusual caught my eye.

In the distance I could see a man in a black track jacket. He continued in a deliberate saunter along the same walkway with his hands behind his back, and then turned around to go back. Along the next parkway there strolled an elderly couple with a Dalmatian; an old bloated bitch. They settled on a bench and the Dalmatian stuck its croup between its master's legs, the dog panting and shaking its pink belly with its nipples that looked like ripple. I saw Victor pass by this group and lite a cigarette, covering half his face with his palm as usual.

"Excuse me, have you got a cigarette?" The owner of the Dalmatian hailed him.

Victor turned. "It's my last one," he replied, and unhurriedly went away towards the highway.

Half an hour later I reached the apartment where Vlad was waiting for us. Victor came up at my heels. He was holding a bag of sausages and French fries.

"Could you give my coat back?" Vlad greeted Victor at the doorstep. "So, what's up there?"

"The coat worked out; they were waiting for you," Victor said. "There was no Meier. But that means nothing at all. Meier could be in trouble himself, or just in debt, so he could have decided to pay them off by selling you out as a key to the deal, couldn't he? So, to whom could he sell you out? Could that be to the public prosecution, right away? He might as well be unaware of the intruder presence, but once he noticed the bank being checked, could he have decided to act with dispatch?"

"We won't ever know. And what should we do with that other appointment; the one with Michael Brown, the embassy interpreter?" Vlad asked in a low voice, as if he was asking this question to himself, for the hundredth time.

"When does he want an appointment?"

"It's the day after tomorrow at the railway station."

"Has he ever asked for an appointment before?" Victor inquired.

Victor tied up his flannel shirt, stirred up the wood coal in the fireplace, and laid the sausages on the roaster.

"Yeah, one time ago he asked me to pay in advance; he was short of money," Vlad recollected.

"He's seen you before and he knows you can arrange things..."

"Yes, and he knows a lot of interesting people, so I prepaid him."

"You can go to his appointment, that is nothing unusual," concluded Victor. "Have you finished off the vodka?"

"I've smoked just about all we had. Every cigarette may be my last one."

At night the whole scene repeated itself again. I woke up from the cigarette smell and from his fingers softly rapping on the keyboard. Vlad was sitting with his laptop, his face looking faded and tired in the screen light.

"Vlad, should I make some coffee?" I asked gently.

As though he hadn't heard, he hardly turned his head towards me. The flare of his spectacles covered his eyes so that he seemed blind.

"I cannot be tracked just by bank transactions," Vlad whispered as if he'd exhausted all other possibilities.

Yes, under close examination, one could see Vlad was money-laundering; but then, it was quite common. Vlad owned two companies in Canada and Israel which in itself could not arouse suspicion. These two companies had founded a third one, an intermediary at its core, here in Germany. This third company was holding an account with Hurst Bank through which they paid their salaries and taxes, and then also they had an account in a Swiss bank.

The intermediaries involved in the deal in question had similar arrangements; sometimes the chain of the agent firms was a bit longer. This normally did not attract unwanted attention.

Some way or another, nobody ever tails people through the city who are involved in money laundering.

"Have you drowned out some cash?" I wondered on my way back from the kitchen, placing a cup of coffee and biscuits in front of him.

"No. Why do you ask?" he snapped.

"Vlad, and how come you've...? I'm sorry." This question had popped out of my mouth of its own accord. I almost bit my tongue.

"Become the informant of Lubyanka office?" Vlad snorted. "I was young, and they set me up easily, as if

I had stolen my company's money. Then later, when I agreed to all their terms, this money would be transferred to my bank account in Geneva so that I'd eventually have stolen it... Hold it. I've got to have a look at that old account of mine in Geneva... Hell," Vlad cursed out discontentedly, his fingers grown stiff over the keyboard as if he was scared, himself, of that idea.

Victor woke up from the boiling kettle noise and came over to stand behind Vlad's back.

"Come on, Vlad, let us have a look there, just in case," prompted Victor.

Vlad entered his password. He had the commonplace name of Harvey Smith and an address in San Francisco. His bank account in Geneva contained twenty thousand dollars. This money had come from Moscow fifteen days earlier, shortly before the tax authorities' visit to the bank.

Vlad grew so pale that the freckles on his face turned even brighter.

"They've burnt me out. I thought someone could track me down, but not quite this way," he whispered.

Victor also froze on site, looking at the screen for a minute.

"Vlad, have you really been dreaming of dying in your own bed? Well, now we know for sure this was not just an accidental piece of crap. Both you and the bank were hit in a single stroke," Victor remarked.

"What should I do now?" Vlad asked this question in a voice so low he seemed speaking to himself.

"Whatever. If you wish, you may straight away go to the US embassy. This may be a better option to choose before they detain you right here," Victor suggested.

"Why have they sold me out? I stopped working for anyone long ago..." Vlad was totally at sea.

Not getting a thing there, I whispered in fear, "The US embassy? Vlad, are you American?"

Later, Vlad told me he had been brought up by his adoptive parents in San Francisco and he did not know who his real parents were. Differently from Victor, Vlad's face features clearly were a hundred-percent German. Or did it only seem to me to be so?

"This payment is a valid reason for his arrest. Money can't lie. Yes, it can be traced if they know about it. This must have already been reported to the embassy. That explains the surveillance. But they were not tracking Vlad Holt, but Harvey Smith," Victor explained to me.

"And what about that appointment Ben Meier never came for? You were thinking they probably expected to make sure they saw Vlad there. What was it, then?" I wondered.

"I guess Ben Meier sold out Vlad as the key to the whole deal, without knowing that Vlad was actually Harvey Smith. Now, follow me." Victor was still contemplating the whole thing. "The guy who paid Ben Meier to call out Vlad for an appointment knew that Vlad was Harvey Smith."

"And who could it be? How could he know this?" I asked him, but Victor only shrugged.

"I can't believe it. How come I'm still sitting here?" Vlad whispered.

Victor patted Vlad on his shoulder. "Send the money back."

"And what do I write in reply: *Go fuck yourself, comrades*?" Vlad gave us a lop-sided grin and then cut himself short. "Hold on, Victor - this interpreter Michael Brown, the one I had to meet, he works for the American embassy. How do you like this shit?"

"Fuck. He had an opportunity to learn about you if... that means..."

Victor and Vlad looked at one another and for about a minute they dared not speak.

"Oh, shit..." Vlad sighed, sitting back on his chair and starting to smoke.

"Come on, Vlad, keep awake. Who may testify against you in court?"

Vlad paused to think,

"It could be just one person, for a fact. He's done this before. He lives in the suburbs of New York City, and he obtained his citizenship over twenty years ago. He's older than me."

Vlad was right. For a trial in a spy case, one could as well do without much evidence. What kind of evidence could there be? Some outdated wireless transmitter with his fingerprints on it? This was ridiculous. More often, the sentence was just based on some defector's testimony.

"Fine," Victor nodded. "I'm packing my things. Vlad, you'll spend a week here with Ann, or whatever time you think appropriate. Just sit still in here and keep quiet. I'll let you know how things are, and will leave you a message as usual. That's it; you'll be waiting for me here," Victor instructed him, and started getting ready to leave.

"What's up? Where are you going?" I wasn't getting it.

Victor was ready in a minute. He was in a hurry and was soon standing at the door with his travel bag.

"Wait till I call you; that'll go off all right. The hell with the deal; we've got to pull Vlad out of this shit now," Victor hissed into my ear as he kissed me goodbye.

"Are you leaving me with this girl over here? She's got neither tits nor butt. She's asking me weird questions." Vlad put on a semblance of still being worried.

"Vlad, she's also got some freckles that may be on her butt, too. Have a closer look, can't you see this? And don't you whimper." Victor gave him a hug, and turning his head to me, he said, "Should Vlad wish to go out some place, you beat his legs."

Victor left. Closing the door behind his back, I stood there benumbed, not understanding a thing.

"Oh, Victor has not even eaten his sausages," Vlad suddenly recollected. "Would you like some food? Well, I've got to have a drink, then smoke, then another drink and another smoke..."

"Don't hurry, get a snack," I smiled perplexedly, stirring the coal to lay out the bread to dry. "I haven't understood a damn thing, Vlad. Could you explain it to me?"

"Sure, but not quite everything." Vlad gave a deep sigh of relief.

I could see him calm down; he was feeling a lot better. His cheeks reddened as he took a gulp of vodka by pressing it to his lips, and he revived.

"So, this money from Moscow gets to your account. And the tax authorities visit the bank... And this surveillance... it should mean..." I started saying, still not getting how to put together two and two.

"Look, I think Michael Brown, apart from his role as a middleman in the deal and as an embassy interpreter, was also recruited by Moscow. And in Moscow they know... Err, fuck, someone must have recollected ... that I live in Berlin, and they sent my folder to this side. Such things do happen. Over here, you know the Stasi Archives used to be forwarded to Moscow and back, and they may well have that file of mine." Vlad lit a cigarette. "Or otherwise, Michael Brown may have seen my files... It might just as well be true. He is actually paid to observe what's happening around...

and he could have recognized me from that old photograph of Harvey Smith."

We could only guess how, after taking a look at the photo in an old case file, he was able to recognize Vlad, the person who'd fixed the issues he'd faced in that deal. None of the intermediaries knew the name under which Vlad was living in Berlin. No one could link him to Vlad without knowing how Vlad really looked. This could be only done by someone who had seen his old photo. It could only be one man: the deal participant; the interpreter. So he must have reported to Moscow that a played-out agent was now in control of the major deal of buying up the African countries' foreign debt, and it was the point for hitting the bank and bringing into play all the incriminating evidence collected over these years, on the partners using the bank services.

But who could it be? Even Victor, after several years' residence in Moscow, failed to find out anything.

"Vlad, there is too much coincidence," I said in contemplation.

"I see things don't match up. It's a load of bullshit. But why, then, has Michael Brown called me out?" Vlad was speaking to himself.

"And Victor..." I did not finish saying it - my guess was terrible.

"Yes," Vlad confirmed with a nod.

We never spoke of Victor again.

CHAPTER SIX

COVER UP THE TRACKS

Vlad was waiting for his arrest. It was hard to look at him. The suspense laid him low. He looked drawn and unshaven, with white bristle coming out on his cheeks and neck, glinting like salt efflorescence on the stones. He was now walking with a velvet tread, speaking in a low voice.

Vlad told me we had to find out whether the police had already visited his apartment, and he went out to make a call to a friend of his. On his way back he forgot to buy food and came in with just a pack of coffee and a carton of mini cakes. He went out again late at night, and when he got back, he told me the police had been to his place and that his friend had not spoken to anyone on his way upstairs to his own flat on the next floor; but on the floor above, he'd heard his neighbors in the stairwell speak of the police visit. Or had it really been the police?

In the evening I noticed Vlad slip from his armchair to stand, spread eagled, blankly staring out the window and blowing out cigarette smoke, and I hastened to face away from him. He was smoking cigarettes absent-mindedly one after the other, spilling ashes onto the floor, his own pants, and into the cups around him. He failed to take a nap. I could not sleep either. I woke up in the middle of the night, pulled my jeans off the back of the sofa, found my cigarettes by groping, and started smoking, looking at his crooked silhouette above the paperwork. He seemed to be dissolving in the dusk.

"Vlad, why aren't you sleeping?"

I looked over his shoulder. The blank pages were quickly filling with his small handwriting. He was making a list of the people who could be impacted by his arrest, of those people dependant on him, and of those in trouble, in case he got taken to the USA. There was another list of companies he was working with, and a separate list of the partners and middlemen to the deal who might know more about him than others, and those who could sell him out as Vlad Holt.

"I don't fancy waking up with strange females." Vlad made a wry mouth and then simply added, "Should you be a female, really…? I wish I could have a rest. I'm damn tired from these three days … I never thought I'd have to recollect all my fucking life there. I was thinking that all this time I'd missed out on something, left something undone, and had no time to… If I forget something, I'll hate myself for it. I've got a feeling this is my last day. I feel so fucking bad. I don't know what tomorrow may bring. Could this day pass by, so I can continue living, somehow?"

"Vlad, are these women, and…?" I wondered, with my eyes fixed on the columns of female and male names, which were written separately.

"Yeah, that happens," he replied ambiguously. "I don't really know what I need."

I knew such things sometimes happened. I had been instinctively looking for a man similar to my own father. I was lucky it turned out to be Ilya. One day my father told me, *Hurry up. Ilya is older than me.* Yet Ilya and I were reluctant to make any changes, as if we would live forever.

And what could we wish for? When sitting by Ilya's side in the evening and smoking on the porch of his house, I realized it was useless to wish for anything else. Everything I wanted to change was altering my own life in such a way that there was no gulf between me and Ilya. Would I like to have a family? No. I wanted to have my own bank, and that was the life Ilya was living. However quiet his life seemed, in essence it was pure adrenaline, and once nipped up, it was beyond human power to reject.

"Why have they given me up at this particular point?" Vlad wondered, as if talking to himself.

Vlad said no more, looking over his spectacles, his face laid with the flecks of the lamp light and deep shadows, his eyes sunken. He seemed devastated.

We were sitting out there till morning, drinking and snacking on those mini cakes he'd brought. There was nothing else in the fridge. Vlad was contemplating things, drinking, and speaking as if to himself. He had nothing but guesswork. He was feeling sick now, as the deal and the bank appeared lost due to an absurd mischance that had happened to him. There was no rage; just frustration and disappointment.

There could be several options. Vlad was casting them about in his mind, smoking one cigarette after another.

The first thing to come into his mind was that Vlad had been sold out by a defector who'd just recently applied for asylum with the USA. But he hardly had such a good memory of these old men, and he would hardly get anything in exchange for an oldie's name. Vlad had been neither here nor there for about twenty years now. With a single whiff, Vlad discarded this idea.

Chances were higher that in the USA they'd recently caught a spy who'd been working for Moscow and was still of value. Everyone carried a price. Everyone seemed to be on sale. This spy was probably of such a high value, they wanted to pull him out at the expense of some other agents. Could it be that Vlad had been sold out by Moscow as a played-out agent in exchange for a recently-caught insider that was worth several people like Vlad? To Moscow, Vlad remained a mere bargaining chip. He was just one of many long forgotten sleepers whom they might only recollect when needed. Moscow had given up their sleeper in a rather simple way, just by releasing his real name; the one he'd lived with in the USA, and then money. There was one good thing: the purpose of the payment did not read as *For Long Service and Good Conduct*. Vlad was taking no big risk: just a few years in prison, that was all.

"No, it's not the one." Vlad started smoking again.

"Vlad, it's not your fault," I said softly.

"Who cares? I won't ever get out of this shit," he snapped, and I closed my mouth.

"Who would ever need Harvey Smith? Hold on there." Vlad checked himself. "Oh, I know that! Oh, shit..."

"So who?"

"The secret service of every country has its own handwriting. In short, all these things happening to me are not for real; they are assumed. This is mere illusion."

"Vla-a-ad... are you ok?" I asked him cautiously.

"Look," Vlad reeled off. "We think I've been sold out by the Russian intelligence to the Americans as sleeper Harvey Smith. Why so? This is not clear. So what do we know for sure? There's been a money transfer from Moscow. This is both evidence and a reason to arrest me. We are thinking the US embassy either received an old case file of mine from Moscow or they were simply informed about me. We are thinking there was a tail after me. We guess I'm about to get arrested any minute, now. True, all of the above are good reasons for us to think so. But isn't it too much, close to me? I mean, everything at the same time? That actually indicates that at least half of this is mere assumption on our part." Vlad said this with uncertainty, as if probing the ground.

"How come?" I wondered, setting my glass of vodka on the table in surprise.

"Should there be three pieces of shit and it's unclear who mucked up, then it must be the English lady," Vlad shrugged. "Have you read the book *Ice-breaker*? It contains the reply to a very simple question; that is, who started the Second World War? There may be three different answers: it could have been Hitler, or it could have been Stalin, or they may have reached an arrangement of sorts. It's written in quite a convincing and beautiful way. However, Suvorov the writer is himself a defector and lives in England, working off his wages, which are paid by the British."

In a word, since there can be three different interpretations of the same event, the British intelligence must have worked on it. This is an imperishable classic.

"Do you think you've been given up by the British?"

"I guess the person who told things about me was a defector currently settled in London." Vlad seemed to be in doubt no longer. "The British sold me to the Americans, and they wish to convince the latter that I'm being done by the Russian side... The British seem to cover up the tracks of that defector. He must be of certain value. Or then, I may be mistaken ..."

"Vlad, this is bullshit. If that's so, than someone must have set up the Russian intelligence. Are you kidding? They could have simply set up themselves, couldn't they? And why? This is crazy."

"However, this may still turn out to be true. The Russian secret service must have actually been used as the fall guy, and since it's only about such a mere trifle as a long-forgotten agent, no one would really pay attention. All in all, it's been the British working on this," Vlad concluded.

Vlad told me that whatever it was, there is a standing rule. There are normally two people, one of them selling out an agent by naming him, and that's about his role; he is well hidden someplace. And there is another guy to witness in court who's right in the foreground, living a common life, and everybody knows he played a defector a deuce of a time ago. Once you know to sort these two, it gets easier to tell where the scent of shit is coming from.

"And what about the money transfer?" I dumbly inquired.

"Do me a favor ... This money trace leads straight to a Moscow bank! It's realistic unless you know that Moscow never does things this way. They've never made any transactions from Moscow. That is too high a risk, as money transfers always attract attention. And then, if Moscow intended to set me up, it could be anything but a wire transfer. They are humble guys in Moscow; they just take a gym bag, pack it full of cash, then carry it across the border and find a banker who asks no questions and never stares into your eyes. The habits of Moscow don't ever change. It's been always this way 'till now. If Moscow pays their agent, the money is kept in his personal account in a bank of Moscow so it never moves. This is not at all Moscow-style. Or otherwise they cover up the money trace the way everybody does; normally by choosing one of a million other ways to avert suspicion from Moscow."

"But you've been truly set up this time," I objected.

"Yes, but Moscow would never sell out their agent that way. It would never really come into their Moscow minds. They simply do it in a different way."

"And what about surveillance?"

I remembered Vlad, pale and scared at the door of this apartment for the first time after having noticed the tail, frozen to the spot and unable to smile.

"This surveillance was intentionally arranged for me to spot it. I've lost all my skills long ago, but then, I never really had any. I'm a financial expert, not a spy. Yes, I had some experiences before, but I don't remember anything. And if it were professional surveillance, I would never really notice. So what they arranged here for me was the kind of tail I'm used to. A bear with a balalaika could just as well be following me."

"And could it be the Americans' job? Shit, they must be seeking to arrest you. Have they got many opportunities over here? They can hardly afford anything better than to just thread on your heels."

"So why haven't they arrested me, then?" Vlad retorted with reason, and then I finally saw there was a grain of truth in what Vlad was telling me. "The Americans can afford to do quite a lot over here. This is their territory, in fact. They feel at home in Berlin."

"And the police?"

"The police could join in at the slightest pretext, to complete the picture."

Yes, something was not matching up. This apartment was a pretty reliable shelter in these desolate quarters, but then they should have found Vlad by now, or could it be something different? What was it all about? Was it pure good luck that Vlad was not yet locked up, or was it a sort of intelligence game? Hardly so.

"You know, Vlad, what you were telling us before seemed way more logical to me compared to the kind of bullshit you are telling me now."

"Uh-huh, do you know how much fucking effort it has taken me?! I've almost cracked my brain to figure it out. Fuck!" Vlad threw off in irritation, pouring himself more vodka.

"Vlad, I'll come to suspect everyone now; even the mini cake..."

"And this vodka is good, so sweet." Vlad was smiling slightly.

Vlad was buying me mini cakes. And initially I was thinking, *It's so very easy with Vlad: for him, this mini cake is nothing but cake.* Vlad was rather broad browed, his sincerity was depreciative, and he seemed to be telling what he was thinking. He must have been kicking off people with this sincerity, and it protected him just like an invisible firewall.

Victor was totally different. He used to undress me with a mere glance, and every conversation with him was like talking in bed. It could be just a single phase, but with the next one I felt like sitting on the cooling bed sheets, watching him leave, saying, *Don't you wait for me, honey bunny.* But with time I got accustomed to being a proper female with him and didn't bother. Victor knew how to tell lies straight into your eyes, and speaking to him was much like a muddy stream that carries all sorts of waste along so it's difficult to withstand. That's why I initially found it not so easy to be with Vlad, but his sincerity turned out to be the most subtle and delicate of lies for which you even felt grateful and was eager to give him thanks. I guess people paid him for this. And then I instantly felt that it was a cakewalk, with Vlad.

CHAPTER SEVEN

OLDER THAN

ROCK 'N ROLL

Hell of a thing. After drinking some vodka with a mini cake, I caught myself thinking I'd stepped into the game where I knew neither rules nor players, unaware of what kind of game it was. It seemed stupid even trying to learn something there. But do I really know enough about agents given up in exchange for other agents, and about surveillance modes? Of the way the secret services work in general? I knew nothing about them.

So Vlad used to be a sleeper recruited by the Russian intelligence in the days of rock 'n roll. Damn it, Vlad could just as well be seducing men, such a sweet boy, well on in years... Yes, I could address a couple of questions to Ilya - he used to work for the secret services - but then, he was older than rock 'n roll. So what was Vlad facing ... the British intelligence? Shoot me up. Holy goodness ... is that all done with satellites, electric appliances, and whatever else they show in those movies?

What was it all for? For the sake of the deal? Oh yes, the thing was as beautiful as a high-ranking whore.

The beauty of the deal was that it was all made of old flour. And every cent of that deal was lying in somebody else's hands. Without knowing the hand that handed over this cent to some other hands, one could learn nothing at all. This deal left no detectable e-trace. It was simple and impossible to hold; it was just like a woman who always stayed with someone else in her search for money. It started in places with no internet, with unsustainable power supplies, and it was going back there. It was just like sand flowing between one's fingers, or just a passing glance.

It seemed I was only now starting to realize the power and beauty of the whole arrangement.

And I knew just one thing for sure. In these wars for money, the accountants always win. It all depended on how good Vlad was in finance. If he was as good in finance as he was sexy, then he had a real chance of getting out of that shit.

The British Intelligence, yeah? To hell with it, I thought with boozy ease, and then asked him out loud:

"Vlad, that means you were sold out by a defector from Moscow who's now in London, is that so? And the man who would testify against you in court would be a different defector from Moscow who's not been living long in New York, wouldn't it?"

"True," Vlad nodded, and screwed up his face, gulping vodka. "Yeah, that defector in London seems valuable enough that the British wish to give the appearance of my being burned up by the Russians."

"Fine," I agreed, having my drink after his. "The main question is, what the hell?! Yeah, supposedly the British did someone a favor and sold you out to the Americans, but what for? Why do they want you?"

"And this might be not the American side..."

"Vlad ... you'd better wind down on that nonsense."

"To your health," Vlad said, and slightly clanked his pownie against mine so the sound of glass echoed in the quiet room. "So what's not clear? I live in Berlin. Do you think it's easy to carry me out to the States?

No. I think I'm wanted right here. But then, how to give me to the German counterintelligence? No way. The only option is do it through the US Service."

"And why?"

"Let us sort this crap into two piles again," Vlad started, then paused and added: "or into three."

Yes, Vlad was here in Berlin, and seeking his extradition as a long-forgotten sleeper in order to bring him to the States for the trial would be costly and difficult. He was probably really wanted right here. But for what purpose? That was not so difficult to figure out. Usually a sleeper like him would make a good witness. Someone may have taken a good post or maybe grabbed a fat piece of the cake, and they wanted to destroy that person or just tarnish his reputation, presenting him as a long-standing Russian. That had a ring of truth. Vlad could testify against someone here, and then he would be taken to the States for a mild sentence that, in any case, should be light. And whether Vlad knew that person or not, it did not really matter.

"It's pretty clear, with Harvey Smith, that it's about his arrest to make him a witness in court on this side, followed by his deportation, another court, and some time in prison. But I'm also Vlad Holt," he started again, as if telling his beads.

"And someone wants to destroy you as a clue to the deal... But who? I would rather think this is an attempt by a Russian company to seize the deal again, the one trading in armaments. They normally use the secret services as they wish. And then also this arrangement seems ideal for arms trafficking..."

"Or something like it." Vlad scratched the bristles on his chin thoughtfully.

"Fine. They clearly wish to destroy you. You are the clue. So why the hell should they turn you into a spy and take you to court, then? Why overcomplicate things ... what for?" I halted.

"Why wouldn't they just catch and rack me till I hand them the whole listing?" Vlad snorted, looking into my sulky face. "Well, it gets them nowhere. The deal has already been sold out by someone. We've got a mole in the deal, and he is getting paid. That guy is informed about many and he must have sold out all the partners - whomever he knew. The information on the participants who used the services of Hurst Bank must have been picked up for years. So the majority of the participants are already known. I've become their target just because I can figure out who this mole is and identify him... Is that clear?"

"Yeah, it's enough to drive me mad."

"Would you like a drink?" Vlad asked me, getting up to reach the fridge.

"Yeah, just a bit. Is there anything left?"

"Yeah," Vlad responded, taking a bottle of vodka, heavily clothed in hoarfrost, from the freezer.

We had another drink.

"The guys haunting me as Harvey Smith haven't been informed about me also being Vlad Holt. And those wishing to destroy me as Vlad Holt actually know that I'm also Harvey Smith, a sleeper. They'll invisibly destroy me by somebody else's hand, under cover of Harvey Smith."

"That's it, Vlad." I stopped him with a gesture. "May I have more vodka? To your health. Go on."

"It gets more complicated further on: the fact I'm Harvey Smith and the name with which I was living here in Berlin is only known to the people in Moscow, and also to that defector who's now in London. Look. This Londoner knows I'm Harvey Smith. But is he also aware I'm Vlad Holt? No. But then, someone in Moscow surely knows this..."

"This interpreter from the US embassy could by chance have learned about you - I mean, Michael Brown."

"No idea. However, I have a feeling that someone else in Moscow had known me as Vlad Holt earlier. Suppose that seizure has been underway for a while, and the intruder is Russian, and all this time they've been collecting incriminating evidence. They could just as well have learned a lot about me, if not stripped me to the skin. But then this Michael Brown pops up... Shit, there can be no coincidence with this kind of story. But he's definitely working for Moscow."

"And who's the intruder?" I wondered.

"No idea. Fuck-up. I'll just have another drink and then go to bed. I can't sleep, damn it all."

The next morning, I felt reluctant to get up, but a hurried rustle made me jump. The door to Vlad's room was half open. I could see dim gray light from under the slit of the door. I feared I'd find the room empty. I jumped up and, opening the door a crack, I saw Vlad hitch up his shorts, stretch his whole rawboned body, somewhat swaying, rub his face, scratch his grown bristles, and then go have a shave.

"Vlad! Where are you going? You should not go out.

Oh shit."

"Do you remember that talk with Victor? Michael Brown could have made this appointment to offer me a bargain," he responded, hastily putting on his jacket.

"You'll get yourself arrested, damn it!" I seized him by his sleeve.

"Who? Brown actually knows I'll get arrested anyway," Vlad replied, forcing my fingers to unclasp. "You must understand: I'm not going to sit here waiting for my arrest, and I may well never see Michael again. If I don't meet him now, I might probably miss the only chance to find out who we are dealing with."

"Are you sure? What if that's a regular call?"

"Then I'll go and find out."

"Vlad!"

"Get off my shlong," he cut me short icily.

"Vlad, if you've got something in mind, tell me," I begged him, realizing that he'd leave and I'd never see him again.

"Fine, you can go with me, but you'll have to sit somewhere and look from afar. An extra pair of eyes can't hurt. I'll make a call to a friend of mine along the way, and he'll pull me out. I'll get back. I promise," he conceded.

CHAPTER EIGHT

ABOVE ALL ELSE

We left the house separately and the same way, apart, we walked along the café tables at the railway station. I noticed Vlad from afar: he was sitting opposite a stout, middle-aged man with a sleepy, crumpled face. When talking, the man repeatedly scratched his bald head which was smooth and bore the dim reflection of the billboard's flecks. He wore a proper business suit beneath his wide-open coat and had a slow-paced speaking manner, quiet and monotonous. When I passed by, I could hear nothing, really. He looked at me sidelong and quickly turned his eyes. It flashed through my mind, *There is something fishy about this gentleman, Michael Brown.*

I moved away, to the opposite side. There seemed to

be no one keeping an eye on Vlad. From a distance I could see Brown suddenly get up and take a step as if he'd blindly stumbled upon a nearby chair, then put it aside with his hand and stumbled again against another chair; that of a man sitting by his side. He apologized without looking and walked away with a drunken gait. I quickly averted my eyes from him.

In a minute, from the far end, a tall and respectable-looking gentleman in a classic coat started towards Vlad. At the same time, from the side Brown had just left, I could hear the sound of footsteps and through the moderate crowd that gathered that side, I could see the aide men running. Vlad stood up. The respectable gentleman passed Vlad, and Vlad mingled into the crowd without looking back.

Some time later, after a tour around the street, I entered the apartment. Soon Vlad came. He brought some foodstuffs, vodka and cigarettes; everything in a quiet and matter-of-fact way as if he was coming home.

"It was a friend of mine, he was to lead me out," Vlad uttered at the doorstep.

"Yes, I got it," I nodded, taking the bags from him. "And what about Brown? Were these men running up to him?"

"Maybe, I didn't see," Vlad replied.

"Vlad, what have you told him? Have you warned him?"

"He understood everything, himself. There are people whose jobs involve saying there will be no more pay. I just told him he shouldn't have informed Moscow about me, so he won't get paid. He must be in debt. It's usually the money that turns them into informants. He had not even thought to check me out. So... yes, I kind of warned him."

"What were you talking about? What did he say? Has he offered you a bargain?"

"No. On the way over I was thinking that no one would offer me a bargain. Last time, Hurst Bank was within an inch of a takeover. This is how they make a bargain offer. Brown is just a pawn."

"So what's the matter?"

"I think Brown recognized me from some old photo and informed the people in Moscow that Harvey Smith was the same person as Vlad Holt. But then, he must have told this to the wrong person, and something went wrong. He probably rushed things."

"Oh, then maybe he does not really work for Moscow."

"He does. He's got it written on his face, along with those peanuts he's getting from Moscow."

"I hope that now, instead of running around the city, you could leisurely have some vodka with me," I said, putting the wieners onto the table. Shooting a rapid glance at Vlad, I realized I was mistaken. Within these few days I'd learned to read his face. "Vlad, holy crap, are you fucked up in the head? Why can't you just keep still?"

"We should freeze the deal as soon as possible."

"I'll break your legs off," I hissed at him in impotent rage, understanding that I would not be able to hold him back.

"If you want you can go with me, I'll buy you a cake," he suggested.

I had to agree. That evening, Vlad phoned all of his friends and the middlemen in the deal, making his way from one pay phone to another. After swallowing a lot of icy air and vodka late at night, we finally fell asleep. I could see that Vlad really felt better, now.

The following day, we met some of the partners. It was nothing out of the ordinary, and Vlad hooked his arm though mine in the park when we passed a paunchy smarty-pants in a yellow track jacket who sported diamond-shaped glasses with blue frames and a three-day stubble. Vlad simply gave him a nod, and in a minute the man turned aside and disappeared.

Another one was a slim gentleman with fallen cheeks and a crooked, vulture-like nose. When he saw Vlad in the distance, he started to smoke his e-cigarette, taking a greedy pull the way heavy smokers do and hardly leering at Vlad before disappearing into the crowd. These were his key partners. They wanted to make sure Vlad was fine. As to the rest, Vlad just gave them all a warning by phone. Some of them asked for a date, but the main thing was that Vlad was in time to caution them all. Another four told him they'd been notified by Victor.

One more night of getting enough sleep seemed to return Vlad to life. It was another day full of phone calls and wandering around the city, but little by little, Vlad managed to freeze the deal. Late at night, he got ready again.

"And where the fuck are you going now?!"

"I forgot to buy a mini cake for you."

Vlad made calls to Canada in the morning and in the evening. He was waiting for Victor's call. Vlad said he was not scared about his own arrest but the anticipation was exhausting, so I thought I'd better not hold him. We stopped at a convenience store and then walked an extra couple of blocks under the cold, burning wind. Vlad made another call and finally heard Victor's voice. Victor left him a message that we should not wait for him. He would be reachable for an indefinite time, so I had to go to Moscow for the documents.

"What does that mean?" I inquired, hiding my face from the wind.

"It means the worst thing. The fall-back option. I'll see you to the airport. You'll take the documents and come back here."

We entered the apartment. I pictured, for a moment, my arrival after this trip to Moscow, when there would be no more Vlad. I felt sick with fear.

"Vlad, I don't want to leave you here."

"Have no fear. They won't arrest me." Vlad brushed me off easily.

"How come?" I wasn't getting it.

"At first I was feeling rather helpless. I'm no agent, but a dinosaur. I was thinking that they could have set up some bugs or cameras that I wouldn't even notice..."

"We're just like rats in here." I squealed discontentedly, looked round the rooms in search of a camera, but I could not detect any.

"There are no cameras; no bugging. There won't be any surveillance." Vlad's voice sounded calm and confident.

"Why do you think so?" I wondered perplexedly.

"That's so as to not frighten away the people I'll be still meeting with. The intruder won't settle down until he knows everyone involved. And in this deal, there are a lot of agents; some of them recently retired and some still active. All these people are quite sensitive to this kind of shit, like surveillance. They'll hear when something goes wrong from miles away and will read it from my gait if I should suddenly get nervous. At the least occasion they will all scatter and hide away like rats."

"So the deal is to withdraw into the shadows..." I concluded on his behalf.

"Exactly so. We may loose someone, but the rest will just play it safer."

"And why do you think they won't arrest you?" I was still lost at sea.

"That's because I'm still standing here with you. I guess they only want me as a witness. But who wants me? It must be the German counterintelligence, since I'm here and not yet locked up. A regular arrest is American-style, and the Germans may as well invite me in for a cup of tea. If it were Americans who wished to lay their hands on me, they would have done it long ago, when this money from Moscow first landed in my account. It stands to reason that these two parties' negotiations are underway."

"Hmm, that rather concerns Harvey Smith; but what about Vlad Holt?" I could not make sense of it.

"The insider who sold out the deal probably wants to eliminate me. He must be scared and pressed for time. But things will settle down and those people haunting me now surely have their own eyes and will soon understand they've crossed each other's road, and will come to an agreement. They have probably started negotiating already. This is about secret services; it can't happen all at once, and it normally involves miles of red tape, but I'm sure the party willing to get ahold of the deal is sure the Russians won't take any risks and eliminate me before coming in view of the alien secret service."

"You are being looked after by the German counterintelligence... You must have been sold to the Americans, which played into the hands of those guys seeking to seize the deal. If you are taken to the States, the whole thing is over. But then, you've been sold to the Americans so they could hand you over to the Germans, and something went wrong there. Fuck 'em all ... see, my brain's blowing a fuse."

"The man who'd sold out the deal must have made a point of eliminating me just to keep himself on the safe side. But then in came Germans, and the intruder realized he'd missed out on something important, and then he retreated to see what eventually happens to me, and also to save his own bacon. Some time will pass and he'll know it's just me and only me: the one who knows everyone else in this deal. I'm sure no one would dare to approach me. I think they will still try to eliminate me, but probably in some more delicate way. There won't be any surveillance."

"And what about arrest?" I still missed the point.

"I bet this will be a cup of tea. They could make me a proposal; most likely to give testimony against someone. And if I refuse to do as they want, they'll lock me up and hello, America." Vlad drew a sigh. "I used to feel so good here; just like I owned the place. I love Berlin."

"Vlad, could you promise me you won't be running around the streets? And..."

"Don't you worry, I've got brains enough to never come back to those apartments of mine. I promise. I'll be just sitting here, grilling sausages and waiting for you."

Vlad went to see me off at the airport. In a café, while waiting for my flight, he pressed a pen drive into my palm and grasped my fingers. He was looking at me as if he wanted to read my thoughts, his glasses, in dim flecks, sticking to my face so I had nowhere to hide my eyes.

"In case something happens to me - arrest, or... whatever it may be ... here's the list. Don't you wait on me; nor Victor. I'm sorry to say this, bunny..." and with him calling me "bunny," something inside me faltered. "You'll be Vlad, now."

We had a farewell vodka.

"Would you like one more?" Vlad offered me another drink.

"Between these documents, there is my passport in the name of..."

"Vlada Holt."

I had another drink. Then I stood up and unwittingly squared my shoulders. Everything had changed. I was a different person now. There was no trace of my former self.

My flight was announced. Vlad hugged me, I gave him a kiss on his hot, prickly cheek and he walked away at a lively pace to mingle into the crowd.

CHAPTER NINE

THE MIRRORS

In the morning, I reached Berlin, and after dropping off my luggage at a small suburban hotel, I walked across several blocks and then cruised around the streets before I finally entered an area of courtyards with abandoned two-storied houses. The air was clear and burned like a glass of vodka. The yard was full of snow, which washed to the house porch. The doorsteps and every flange of the front door were piled up with snow. The steps were level, so I had to find them by probing. A deafening silence reigned here, probably due to this snow plastering the dark windows and the void inside.

On the way over, I was afraid I'd find the apartment empty. When I made it upstairs, I breathed in the cigarette smoke mixed with the humid, stale air, sweetly smelling of the old house's decay and brick rubble, which meant that Vlad was there.

"Vlad!" I called out, after I opened the heavy old door into the smoky rooms.

"There is something off-key," he uttered, and waved me nearer.

Vlad looked bewildered, but I could read nothing from his face, with his eyes behind the narrow lenses lit with the screen's glow. Vlad turned the laptop so I could have a look.

There was a short message saying that a Russian defector, someone who had, twenty years back, applied for US political asylum, had died in his house of heart attack a month ago.

Vlad had thought that this particular Russian defector could testify against him in court. And now it turned out the prospective witness had died before they'd had a reason for Vlad's arrest. They never hasten to inform people of such news. It could be this man had been dead for a long time. Of course, they could easily find another witness, but this one for sure was no longer able to testify against Vlad.

Yes, it felt weird indeed. Could it be a coincidence?

"This death notice must be the inevitable response to the news of an arrest. That is, the arrest of one spy followed by the sudden death of another. But I actually found no wire about the arrest."

"Do you think they killed the man?" I wondered, even if it seemed quite clear.

"I guess someone found himself in a situation similar to mine just a bit earlier. And this other guy was aware of his imminent arrest, or he'd been warned about it. As to who could testify against him, he could have also guessed it just, like I did. There could not be many witnesses able to testify against a sleeper who formerly worked for the Russian intelligence over twenty years ago, could there? And thus, a month ago, this prospective witness died … The turncoats usually have no common deaths." Vlad stopped talking. He took out a cigarette and turned to the window. "I guess they only needed me to replace that dead witness in court. I was in the States at the same time, I'm about the same age, and, as such, I'm of no real interest to them." Vlad started smoking. "That means, I'll be next."

It seemed unbelievable. Was it a mere coincidence? Or could we have missed something there?

Yesterday night in Moscow I'd opened the envelope to draw out an Estonian passport with a photo of mine, but this was not me but another woman, Vlada Holt. Along with the passport there was a marriage certificate and a change of name certificate, some documents for the offshore companies, and a driver's license. Vlada Holt was very much a real person.

My future suddenly seemed crystal clear. In that future, my name was Vlada Holt and I had a husband named Vlad Holt, whom I'd met four days earlier in this deserted house.

So what was the matter? Who could have recollected that Vlad used to be an agent, twenty years back? Who would need him as a long-forgotten agent? No one would, really. It appeared ridiculous. Vlad had long forgotten that fact himself as, in essence, he had never really worked as such. He had been working all this time in an auditing firm in San Francisco. Yes, he used to be an auditor, and he was able to damage the interests of the United States some twenty years ago. But one had to provide proper evidence. This would be not so damn easy. And then, they had to produce a witness.

As to witnesses, that seemed a lot easier. They could find some kind of elderly Russian defector who had since long been living the quiet life of a common man. Vlad had an idea of who could play that role. But then, once he'd thought about such a man, the man had turned out to be dead.

After a few nights of making lists of the people he knew, Vlad now thought that there was only one person who would be able to testify against him.

Basically, they arrest people only if they have a live witness. Otherwise, anything else such as self-indulgence, suspicious bank transfers, and promenades in front of the Russian embassy with a laptop or a doggie would not really count. Neither conversations nor dates with the Russians would do. The court could only accept the words of someone who had, in the same period, worked for the Russian intelligence and could thus confirm that Vlad had been also recruited. It was normally done by some defector. Should the opportunity arise, one could give testimony in court. Had this dead turncoat really known Vlad? It was of no importance. Could the defector Oleg Lyalin be acquainted with one hundred five agents? Of course not; that was out of touch with reality. However, all of them were deported from the UK.

It mattered only they could have a flesh and blood witness in court to testify against Vlad.

Might this situation have a mirror image so that Vlad now found himself in the shoes of that dead defector?

"Vlad, do you think they burned you up just to make you testify against someone else?" I wondered, looking into his eyes to see my own face iced in fear in the blind flecks of his glasses.

Vlad nodded. We had already discussed this. It seemed to be a clear explanation for everything. Vlad could see no other reason. Why else would they need a long-sleeping agent? He said this was quite common. In case he did not know the man against whom he had to give testimony, they would simply hint to him the name of the right person which he was supposed to recollect.

It must be a similar, long-forgotten agent; someone well advanced in years who had probably taken far too big a piece of the cake or exposed himself too much.

But now this long-forgotten agent was not just keeping still and waiting for his arrest, but was seeking to identify and kill prospective witnesses. He was right, in his own way. In every world there are certain rules, including in business, politics, and espionage. And the people agree to these rules when choosing this or that world for themselves. In the past, traitors used to be executed. Nowadays, they somehow live into old age, getting social benefits and making their little businesses. The traitor, till the end of his days, would keep doing it the way he used to; that is, continuing to betray people he did not even know. Ten to one, he does not know them, but as to the people he used to know and who also used to know him; he must have betrayed them from the start so that they could not sell him short. This is the simple logic of treachery.

So, once the word leaked out, Vlad could serve as witness against this person. Vlad's death would be just a matter of time.

Would Vlad be the next dead witness? Was it really so?

The fear came up into my throat. My body seemed to melt and weep under my skin like a snowball. I glanced at Vlad. His face was pale and stiff, as if something had already died inside. And I thought that while it was not the first time he knew his death was looking for him, he was able to protect himself from that fear through this kind of chilly distancing. It also meant liberty; otherwise this fear, the scariest fear of the unknown, would have ruined him.

It seemed impossible that he could have allowed for all possibilities, only to come to this very end.

"No, Vlad, could it be that...? And who could provide evidence of you being a Russian sleeper?"

"That money transfer from Moscow should be enough."

Vlad said it was such a mess, they could have easily taken away his case file and brought it straight to the US embassy.

"What does that case file look like?" I wondered.

"It could be a simple data card," Vlad replied.

This case file, even if it was really there, had probably played no part in matters. I asked why Vlad had not been given away earlier by any of the turncoats, when a wave of those Russian defectors had flooded the West. He had no clue. He had worked there not long after his career took off, until he was invited to move to Germany and his documents were probably sent to the Stasi. Or were they forwarded there for real? Everything crashed in a blink, the connection was lost, and he seemed to have been forgotten by everyone.

So where could these documents be, at this time? They could be anyplace. But who would need these documents now, if in Germany alone there were over four thousand living Stasi workers on welfare, not to mention another half a million stoolies? The case file, as such, cannot really go places on its own accord. Someone has to bring it in, and this someone normally becomes a witness. There should have been a witness. If his case file turned up out of the blue in the US embassy, it would appear to be nothing but a fake.

Since Vlad had not yet been arrested, there was probably still no witness to confirm that Vlad had been recruited while living in the States. And the Germans did not really want another spy scandal, and could it be that the witness had not come to Berlin for that reason? Vlad told me the Germans who had been working for the Stasi earlier generally preferred to live on their modest pensions rather than play stoolies for some other secret services.

Vlad said that things were not matching up, indeed. His being a former agent was still a point to prove. If he were in the States, it would have been somewhat easier; but he was here in Berlin. Per the documents, Vlad was a German citizen and he would remain German until they could duly prove he was the American, Harvey Smith. And only from that point on would he be entitled to testify against someone else. Would it not be easier to just to find another defector who had lived for long time in the US; someone writing reminiscences on the Lubyanka? There would be no need to prove anything, then. It would be well known and clear that the man used to be a spy, and he would not refuse to give testimony, as there was no way they would ever accept his refusal to do so.

So was it worth seeking evidence that Vlad had been an operative some twenty years back? Who would ever need a long-sleeping agent? It was not enough for them to prove he'd been a former agent. They also had to present evidence that he had diminished the security of the United States of America. Of what damage could one speak of now, twenty years later, with him having lived in Berlin all this time?

"Vlad, and what if ... you come to the US embassy. How soon could they find out you used to be Harvey Smith?" I asked.

"They would not. Everything was properly cleared after my departure. My parents were my adoptive parents. And I left the country twenty years ago. There is no record."

Vlad said one could easily tell which year he had been recruited, and by whom. This was like a seal a man carried forever. This print was usually left by the place where these had people lived and studied, worked, and received treatment. This was exactly what they were looking for. As to the years in question, there were no clues left. Nobody knew the agents that used to contact him. The agents at that time had reported to no one, really. The recruiting agent was free not to tell management about the people he'd recruited. Those who knew the name of a valuable agent were called back to Moscow right away in order to prevent any accidental leaks. That is, only three to four people could really know about any particular agent. So Vlad thought that everyone aware of him had died by now. There was neither paperwork nor fingerprints, or anything else, left behind.

"Vlad, there are probably friends or a girlfriend."

"All of them think I died, and they are kind of used to thinking so, after twenty years."

"Vlad, anyway, someone has to be a witness. Why the hell would they burn you up if no one at all could prove that you used to be a spy?" I wondered.

"They could offer me a bargain. My confession and testimony against someone they want in exchange for a decent prison and a mild espionage term."

"And you?..." I checked myself. One could not really refuse a bargain. Such refusal cases could be counted on fingers.

Two days earlier, we had thought Vlad had been burned up so that he could give testimony against someone right here in Berlin. If there had been someone of high value, such as an American citizen, they would have just taken him to the States and sentenced him there. In that case, they could easily find a turncoat witness in the States and could have brought that recently-dead defector to Berlin. It would have been easier than proving that Vlad was a former operative. It would be far more difficult to bring Vlad abroad. That meant that Vlad would have to testify against someone German, so the man would be judged in Germany. The Americans could only provide some evidence that the man had formerly lived in the States at about the same time as Vlad, and thus had damaged US national interests when he was recruited by the Russians. It seemed a questionable venture, but then, could that other man still be worth it?

Two days earlier, we had thought the worst thing to happen would be his arrest. Vlad would be pressured to testify against someone, and if he refused, he would receive a mild sentence for espionage. All evidence seemed to be pointing in that direction.

I wondered,

"Vlad, have you ever been thought about what would happen if one day you go back to the States?"

Of course he had. He would spend two years in prison and walk free, and then he would also get back some part of his former life.

"It seemed to me, earlier, that if one day there came an angel to tell me, *Should you wish, you may drop everything and run from here in your bare skin up to San Francisco,* I would run across all those States, flinging up my old bare ass. But I'm actually afraid I would have run to there only to find no one waiting for me on that side."

Vlad did not tell me that coming back to his former life would be as good as death to him. There could be no former life. All his life was here in Berlin now, and he was ready to give anything for this life of his.

"I've been here for twenty years and I saw the Berlin wall falling, I've passed here through joy and sorrow, I've got friends here, and this is my city. I have no wish to go back. I know there is nothing left of my San Francisco. I have no wish to fool myself: this is all a mere illusion," Vlad added, taking a gulp of vodka and pressing his lips. "But at times I can see my San Francisco in my dreams."

Vlad told me he knew the people who'd made it back to the States and others who went back to the Soviet Union. Upon their return, they'd realized they'd come to the wrong country. It was not quite the world they used to live in before. Everything seemed alien to them and they could see no place for themselves in that other world.

It took some of them years to get back to the world they had escaped earlier, and upon return, it deceived them, as it was nothing more but a might-have-been happiness; a mere ghost. For some of them, the cost was rather high as they realized that however badly they felt in this strange land, they were forced to go to on with life because in their home country, it was way worse.

For me, it was somewhat similar. Recently I had a feeling that the remnants of the Soviet Union were starting to rise from the ruins to rebuild into skyscrapers. They said it was nothing like the old Union, but was a new world, and that the former USSR was gone beyond retrieval. This was probably true, but I still had a fear of going back into that past. As the years rolled by, I was not able to change and kept reliving the time of the collapse.

I loved it so much; the putrid smell of the giant empire! It was the smell of freedom. Would I like to go and find it somewhere else? No, it would be too naive to think so. It was nowhere else to be found. I seemed to have lost myself. I continued living, somehow, among those other alien people in a strange city. Many contacts of mine were gone from my full belly lifestyle, and those who remained were scarce; they seemed to visit me from someplace afar. They were like ghosts of my former life.

I was a ghost, myself, hooking onto my memories with all my might only to find mere void under my fingers. People used to tell me I was living in my own illusionary world, but I was ready to pay any price for this illusion. The thing is: those coming back to the former Union would not be able to cut out a place for themselves. They would not fit in there.

God damn this Vlad. I felt reluctant to think about it, let alone talk to him about it. He had a pretty good understanding of all those things.

Right now this kind of conversation seemed a happy illusion. Of all things, Vlad and I had been sitting here in the kitchen just two days back, drinking vodka with mini cakes and thinking that the worst thing that could happen to Vlad was over. We had been so mistaken! That option was no longer possible. The death of the defector changed everything all at once.

"Would you like a mini cake?" Vlad asked me.

"A mini cake? Vlad you've been out again; oh my fucking god... Why the fuck you aren't sitting still?" I started hissing at him in impotent rage, fully aware he could not keep hiding here for long.

"I knew you would be back soon," Vlad shrugged.

"Vlad, do you know I'm your wife?" I wondered.

"I guessed so," he replied ambiguously, avoiding the discussion.

I looked at myself through his eyes. He was rather patient with me, probably understanding that we might spend God knows how much time in this apartment together like rats in a trap. I was thinking, *Oh, my God, how long could I be his wife? Could you make it endless, O Lord?*

"Vlad, you told me the guy who knows about you is in London and he won't testify against you. This seems logical to me. Though, what logic can we talk about, here? I'm not getting a thing from this damned weird life ... You could refuse. Oh God, do they really want to get a confession out of you? But you can refuse, can't you? What have they got against you, apart from the words of that defector whom they won't let out of London? It could be nothing at all."

I glanced at Vlad and I could read from his face that he would have no chance to refuse. He took another cigarette and, with his face to the window, said through his teeth, "Don't you be so naive. I'll have to sign my confession. However…"

"Vlad, you are not a common American; you are a Russian agent. It would not cross their minds to make you sign this confession," I suggested, and then I could see on Vlad's face that he was also thinking of something like that.

"I'm an accountant. I can't remember any of those game rules. Anything I say is my guesswork only," Vlad said, a wry smile slightly twisting his lips.

"Where have you gotten this from?"

"All those partners are different. Some of them tend to hog the blanket. There is never an open threat. They just let you read it, somehow. I'm used to reading an implicit threat in every gesture - in every mini cake, that is." Vlad wanted to smile, but he could not.

We stopped speaking and stayed there, smoking in silence, looking out the window. The evening shadows floated, turning pale to transparent, and disappeared into the buildings' shade as if into water. Then darkness lit the yard, raising up to the roofs and delicately contouring in snow-like white the tops of the roofs and the branches of the old poplar trees, like a black and white photo. I felt somewhat uneasy that the window's golden light didn't cover the snow. It seemed that everything had already happened, with just a print left on that photo. Or maybe it had not, but the print would remain for a lifetime. The fear is always imprinted; etched in memory and on the person's face.

"Shit. Vlad, there must be professionals who'd be able to hide you. I'm sure that among those contacts of yours, there is someone," I suggested.

"Not from the British Intelligence, mein herz. I have no one to ask."

CHAPTER TEN

THE DEAD TRACE

At night the wet snow filled the yard between the houses, pasted up the windows, and, when it was a bit melted, started leaking down the glass like thick syrup. From under the white snow the windows of the deserted apartments became even darker, the flecks no longer hiding the depths of the emptiness inside. The rooms turned gray and lifeless and dull, the sounds became thudding noises and the silence came full on, as if the house had sunk underwater. There was not a single trace on the yard pathways. From the half-open kitchen window I could hear the sound of wet snow.

"There is so much solitude here," Vlad remarked, looking out the window.

"Vlad, do you ever sleep?" I wondered, taking a seat by his side to smoke a cigarette, and noticed that Vlad had not been sleeping. He looked peaked and clueless. "Do you remember that other time when I was thinking it was the British intelligence underway?" he asked, placing in front of me a saucer with a mini cake and a cup of coffee.

"Yeah. That time you said that if there were three answers to one simple question, this one would be of the British Intelligence's hand. That's classic," I nodded.

Vlad had returned to thinking the British Intelligence was protecting the man who'd sold him out by clearing him of suspicion, to ward off the trail to Moscow.

"Uh-huh. I'm over-simplifying things, but in essence, the situation is this way, and there is more to it. I've been thinking all this time of that dead defector." Vlad was still contemplating, as if finding his way. I could hear perplexity in his voice. "There is more to this classic. The dead ends are another classic feature of British Intelligence."

"How come?"

Vlad said that sometimes they spoke of certain events that looked finished and evident fact, also confirmed by some known expert opinion, by an archive transcript or by something else, no matter what... It is also notable that such a professional often gives his opinion right before his own death, so there is no way to check it out. It's quite difficult to make your way through the archives. The rest seems scattered across several other sources; the paths to which, again, are rather long and labyrinthine. No one is really trying to convince you of anything. There are no lies or related-party interests. This is why you don't really notice right away that these are all dead ends. This presentation style is typical for the British Intelligence, to put it in simple terms. It is their signature. This is their classic approach, which never changes over the years - or maybe even for centuries...

It took me some time to realize Vlad was speaking of the dead defector, and I froze with a barely-lit cigarette in my fingers.

"Hold on, Vlad, do you think this Russian defector who died of heart attack in New York... I'm not really getting it... What's the point?" I inquired, trying to guess something from his stiff glance, but he seemed to be speaking to himself.

"It's all about the dead ends. Suppose the British Intelligence clears their suspicion of the defector who knows me; and not just me but someone of higher importance. The defector has a certain value. Then clearing him of suspicion actually means taking the trace to somebody else," he concluded.

"I'm not getting it. What are you talking about?"

"The trace can hardly lead to nowhere. It should take you to some real person. The trace should bring you to somebody. And this person would turn up dead. This is how the British work. This is what one should expect of them."

Vlad was telling his own thoughts, his glasses propped on his forehead, and he stared at me unseeingly. He started smoking nervously and then turned away to the window. In the reflection of the window, gray with the morning light, I could see his seemingly lifeless face distort, his glance stiff and haunted.

"Erm, and there we have that dead man... I haven't got it, Vlad. I'm not getting a damn thing! Not a fuck! What do you mean?!"

"Look. I'm nil. I'm of no value to the people who burned me up. There is someone valuable who is in a situation similar to mine, and the man probably got there a bit earlier. The defector in London spoke about him. This is the man against whom the dead defector from New York should have testified. The defector from London was to be hidden. But how could they do it? Instead of him, they could give away someone else; some other agent formerly working for Moscow. It could be a dead man. This dead man would be me. And I've been contemplating why the hell they would take all this trouble with me, haven't I? No, they don't need any trouble. There is no need to arrest me, carry me out to the court, or secure any confession of mine. They can simply kill me. And the perfect evidence of my being a former agent would be that money trace from Moscow. I would make a dead man with irresistible evidence; a self-murderer with a letter of contrition where I'd tell of being recruited along with some other people whose names I'd list in the same letter. This is classic. This is how it works."

I froze. I was struck by this simple thought. How could Vlad think this way? Was he really used to thinking and living with such thoughts?

Once this idea came into his mind, Vlad could not get it out of his head and move forward. It looked so simple and self-evident. He was smoking with his elbows spread on the table, holding his cigarette right in front of his face and hiding his wry mouth and stiff glance behind the smoke. I remembered seeing him do the same thing when he'd just noticed the tail.

"No, Vlad! No... Then this defector from New York would be still alive. Why would the British kill him? If the British wished to hide the source that had pointed at someone else while covering your dead body, why would they have killed the witness; that other defector from New York? They probably have a different task, which is giving away someone while hiding their source. Suppose they have given someone of value to the Americans. And the Americans had a ready witness against the latter. Why would they have killed that witness? There is no logic in this."

"The witness could have been taken care of by the agent himself; the one awaiting his arrest, as I told you earlier. He is an agent, not a dog's dick. Yes, he's about my age and has long been inoperative, but should the need arise, he could still remember how to do these things. It's irrelevant who actually gets to kill me; the British Intelligence or the man who killed the

defector. I would rather place my bet on the British."
Vlad waved the smoke away.

"Vlad, the man whom the Americans want to charge with espionage is a separate thing. He might have killed the witness. But there is no reason for the British to kill that witness."

"What if the British are not covering for him?"

Vlad said this as if he was thinking about it or knew it could happen this way; as if speaking about a possible move in a chess game. He seemed to be casting about in his mind for all the possible options, and none of them looked new or unexpected to him.

"Covering? A Russian agent? The British? Then why are they selling him out?!"

"They may have been forced to do so."

Vlad said this with ease, as if moving a piece on the checkerboard.

Oh God, it was just like talking in a madhouse. I failed to understand the simplest things. Why would they accuse anyone of espionage? Couldn't there be any other charges for a man of his age? Since he was an American citizen, would not it be logical to charge him for tax evasion? And he would rot in jail all the same. Why should they pry up that old espionage crap, which is hard to find out and even harder to prove?

Vlad reluctantly explained that the man had probably lived in the States before, and he was living in Berlin nowadays. This was the only explanation for the fact that they had found nothing else to charge him with. Otherwise, they could have given consideration to some other charges - yet something was missing. And a case of espionage would not really attract much public attention. It would, rather, be taken for granted, just like tax evasion. Or maybe they wished to blackmail someone with that kind of charge. The latter was more likely.

As to the Russian defector in the UK, he would never appear in court and would not turn up at all. They say the Russian secret services do not really hunt defectors, but this is not quite true; they are hunted and not many of them survive, or the above statement may be limited to those who work for two different parties. So there were probably valid reasons to hide the man.

Vlad had come to Berlin twenty years ago, and he had long since forgotten that he used to have a friend, once, who'd made him an agent by just making him sign a receipt for the money he'd been handed, plus going to a few meetups. All of this had been long since forgotten. Who could remember him? How could it have happened? That friend of his has long since died, but his name was probably somewhere on file or within the recollection of someone aware of that recruitment fact. But who could it be? Vlad thought that all of them had died. And it probably had nothing to do with the records. Who would have been digging into these miles of records and listening to thousands and thousands of hours of audio recordings to learn something of an agent who had been recruited so long ago that he could no longer recollect it himself?

One could only learn about such an agent from the words of another agent. And that kind of person had turned up. Vlad used to think he was holed up in the UK, but judging by the events of the last few days, which we'd had to spend in this apartment, the British Intelligence was involved. Everything was staged. The way Vlad had been sold out to the Americans by his own friendlies; that comes from the Russian secret services. This seemed quite common these days; nothing to note. But not to Vlad.

All of these things happening to Vlad now could not be anything but of someone's making, to make that money transfer from Moscow alone... Well, Moscow never makes bank transfers. It would simply never enter their minds; not even the morning after. They'd acquired no such habit, and their habits never really change. In Moscow they are used to catching an agent in the act. This is the golden rule of Moscow, and it means they give their agents away in the same ways, caught in the act with an old transmitter or a few kilograms of secret paperwork on their hands, or maybe also with a pack of doughnuts, to invite publicity.

"Vlad, are you sure you are of no value?" I asked him dubiously.

"That's for sure. The person involved cannot be unaware of it. There would be some hint, otherwise. All these things happening here have nothing to do with me, but swirl around another person who's wanted by everyone and who used to be an agent. He might have stolen a piece of cake or something. And I've got nothing that could be of any interest to the secret service. Even if I had, why would they have exposed me this way when it would be so much easier to just kick the crap out of me?" Vlad shrugged. "That only means they wish to use me either as a witness or to gain my proper confession in court, or have my dead body and a confession."

This is why Vlad believed they had burned him up; not because of the deal. If someone had really wanted to get the full list of the partners to the deal from him, they would have kicked the crap out of him. Whatever it was, there seemed to be no point in making a spy out of him.

"Vlad, I'm not getting it. Why would they give the man to the American services if the man is about to slip through their fingers, since the witness is dead, there is no evidence, and he can just walk away? Do you really believe it? What does it look like? Could it be true?"

"Anything can happen. Sometimes two parties strike a bargain. Say that one party wants to have their defector back in Moscow and the other has to agree and release him. And they do release him, but as a dead man," Vlad answered with reluctance.

From Vlad's words I could see that the British had involuntarily sold out some agent to the Americans and were now covering him with this witness's murder. And then they would kill Vlad to conceal that source of theirs. If the matter came to trial, the Americans could ask the British to disclose their source, and the British would not do so. Instead, they would release Vlad's dead body along with his dying confession. This bore the stamp of truth. Oh my God. What is wrong with this fucking world?!

Vlad started smoking. I could see that he'd processed the same thoughts somewhere deep inside.

He told me the British services do their work as gracefully as the artist paints a portrait. The last moment is when the artist puts a fleck in the eye. And the whole picture is made for the sake of that ultimate stroke. The artist cannot do without that fleck, since this fleck in the eye will instantly revive the portrait. The British do the same. The dead man in the end is a must, whether you want it or not, just because this is their style.

"That's fucking classic. That is, whether I sign my confession of being an ex-Russian spy or not, either way, it will end up with this dead body of mine." Vlad was breathing out smoke into the half-open window, looking at it melt in the damp morning air.

"No, Vlad! This is bullshit. Not all of them here are really good artists. Nope... Vlad, you should escape! Clear off at once! I'll handle it on my own."

"Not the British Intelligence, mein herz. I already told you this." Vlad replied with his lips only.

Was it really so? Could a person so easily see through his own death? Does it really unveil its face in that simple way?

Something seemed wrong here. I was running from clear-cut answers. The whole of this fucking world is made the way every question may be answered: with two interchangeable yet quite opposite answers. This was life, and this is how it works. I always had two different answers. Or maybe this was the reason why I'd chosen the role of the middleman, and I felt somewhat better when looking at things from the sidelines. So, where was the second answer?

Otherwise, if Vlad was not mistaken and the British Intelligence was involved, there might even be three different answers. Or more?

Yes, to the secret services, Vlad was a small coin. It seemed in reality that everything revolved around some other man who appeared important to all those parties, and someone had warned the man of his possible arrest. Vlad now thought of himself as Harvey Smith. That man had died long ago. However, he could now come back from oblivion due to some old paperwork kept in dusty archives and put to death the real man, Vlad Holt.

"Vlad, do they specifically need you? You could escape, just disappear, and they'd have to find someone else instead. Do you really think they would be looking out for you somewhere in Australia where you could take the job of a kangaroo herder?" I could make no sense of it.

No, really, why should it be Vlad? Vlad actually knew nothing and was of no value. And the day before, we'd thought Vlad was wanted as a live witness only. Or did they not want him alive anymore? Then, could they just use him as a cover with the legend *The dead man says so?* He would be a poor witness.

"Or maybe what they need is a poor witness," Vlad said.

"That's it, Vlad. That shit is fucked up; it's not good enough... Shall we have some vodka?"

CHAPTER ELEVEN

CRANBERRY VODKA

Until this point, Vlad had been recollecting all of his contacts night after night, filling the pages of a notebook with his minute handwriting. Waking up in the middle of the night, I could see his silhouette and his smoldering cigarette light through the door's open crack. He kept writing down the names of the people who used to work by his side at his audit agency in San Francisco, but he could not remember anyone making a notable career for himself; the kind people can't really make without third party assistance similar to what Vlad had achieved.

He could see no one there.

Who could Vlad possibly testify against in court? Who was that person who had been recruited at about the same time as he? Did the man happen to be somewhere nearby? It could be an influential politician or a businessman whose reputation they expected to tarnish. Why not? His career would be ruined as soon as the people saw he'd been recruited by the Russian Intelligence a deuce of a time ago, and then frozen at the time of the big mess. No one would be surprised by this news. They had probably collected enough damaging evidence on that man, but this was nothing without a live witness.

Who could it be? Likely someone who expected to be arrested. But who?

Today Vlad stopped searching through his memories. It now seemed useless. What difference could who he recollected make, to his death note?

"Vlad, yeah, it may be true that the British gave the man to the Americans and straight away knocked him out of their hands by leaving them with a dead witness and, possibly, with an equally dead source." After a gulp of cigarette smoke, I had a coughing fit and found it hard to speak. "But you said that the German counterintelligence wants you. What the fuck... Why so?"

Vlad paused to think and pulled the saucer with the cake closer to him, then reached for another cigarette. While lighting it, he started slowly breathing out the words: "The British Intelligence has given that man ... hmm, to the Americans? We don't know this. And me to the Germans? Could be true. But the Germans aren't aware they will be getting a dead man."

The fact that the British had given him away not to the US but to the German secret service was obvious to Vlad. Vlad had been delivered to the Germans through the Americans.

I asked him why was he so sure.

Vlad said the US services normally worked in a different way. Vlad would have been tracked, by now. He was an American citizen, so at first they would have tried to call him back to the United States on some kind of pretext or would have carried him out of the country by any means whatsoever; even as part of the luggage. Sometimes a man drinking a can of Coke could later wake up on board an aircraft on the verge of landing at the airport in New York, fully handcuffed. Everyone found it hard to work in foreign territories. Or they could have arranged some kind of trap on this side.

"What kind of trap?" I wondered.

"I could have been approached by a dude speaking decent Russian, wearing Gucci shoes, for instance, and he would have offered for me to have some vodka and then go back to the States to work for the Russians there, just like in the good old days. He would have probably named an old communication agent of mine and handed me a stack of cash." Vlad gave me a wry smile. "Some people get caught this way, sometimes. The conversation is usually recorded. The panels no longer believe in that bullshit, but things never change."

"But how can you keep on the windy side?" I inquired.

"The password. I do remember it. But then, if someone ever tells me this password... I'd simply call the police, that's all." Vlad brushed my questions aside.

There was nothing like that. There was also no arrest, even with that airtight trigger they had duly prepared, the money transfer from a Moscow bank to his real name's account. This made Vlad think he was actually wanted by the German counterintelligence. The British had kindly procured him. It took Vlad a while to guess he'd been given up by the Russian defector and delivered to the British services.

However, the British had hardly had a chance to place him in a coffin. Why so?

Presumably, the case of espionage had not reached the court, and it was only being used for blackmail purposes. Once the matter reached the court, the British would be asked to disclose their sources, and at that time Vlad would probably have a car accident or take his own life.

Could we have missed something? We had thought Vlad was only needed to testify against a similar sleeper agent. We guessed the man was of German nationality and the proceedings were to be held on this side, also. He would be accused of having been recruited by the Russian secret services when living in the States. The witness was dead, now, so they started looking for Vlad, who could replace the man.

Otherwise, why would they need Vlad? We could see no other reasons up to this point, until Vlad found a simple and clear explanation. The British could artlessly cover their source with his dead body. They had enough evidence and there was no need for any confession on his part.

Yes, if required, one could draw up the confession statement and have it mailed to the Russian defector in the

US, in addition to his memories of the Lubyanka. This seemed to be the best solution. As if taking an acknowledgement from a former agent who'd been through the Russian school would be a stupid hard problem.

"Do you remember I told you the arrest is not quite German-style; they would rather invite you for a cup of tea? Why the hell are they not coming with that invitation?"

"And how could they know of this apartment of ours?" I asked a silly question.

"You wouldn't really notice anything, for sure, even if there was a goat with an accordion following you." Vlad could hardly smile.

"Why do you know that?" I felt piqued.

"I was following you. You could have looked into the shop window... You don't really do a damn thing and you could haul in anyone here."

It was not likely. From miles away, one could see I was not a German; so in broad daylight I walked at my usual fast pace, which I became used to doing while living in Moscow. This was a quiet suburb; a small provincial town where no one was ever in a hurry. And if someone had walked as fast as I did, I would have noticed. When entering the building's front door, I usually went up to the deserted apartments on the first floor, and then sneaked back to have a look to see if someone was following me. Yeah, shit, I had not noticed Vlad, that time.

"Vlad, nobody wants me here. They need *you*."

"True. If nobody comes tomorrow, I will be disappointed. I'll have to go for a walk. On my way, I could buy you a mini-cake. Oh, do I really have to go to the police station myself to check on why the hell the police paid a visit to my flat? Well, let us now have a nap," Vlad uttered, getting up and stretching his back.

"Vlad!" I almost burned myself when I accidentally touched him while collecting the cups. "You've got a fever. Can't you feel it, yourself? You must have caught a cold from sitting by the window."

Vlad touched his forehead. His weather-beaten face was dry and hot, floating with red patches, and the bristle growth on his face was now more visible than ever.

"No, I'm just a bit shivery. Shit, I've drunk too much vodka, so aspirin won't work on me."

"I'll make you a vodka on cranberry. It will soon pass. Fuck, where can I get cranberry in the middle of the night?"

"Yeah, that should work fine. I'll get switched off and have some sleep. I'm a bit tired. So go bring me anything you want. What do you treat your husband with?"

"He's never sick. He's a banker. I guess he's just got no time for illness."

"He is seventy-five, isn't he? And..."

"Yes, it stands straight up, with him. I don't know what the gimmick is. One day he called me and said he'd caught a cold. When I came to him, he was already on his feet. He is said to have buried four of his vice-presidents while he was only sick with a cold just once, himself. And I also cure myself with vodka. So try to get some sleep. I'll be back soon."

I recollected Ilya. When taking a pack of documents from Ilya's hands, I told him Vlad had decided I would be Vlad from that point on.

"He did not really want it," I said.

"You want it. Go ahead," Ilya replied.

Before parting, I smoked a cigarette in his company and had my coffee on the verandah. His kiss was hot and bitter.

I suspected all this bullshit I struggled to push away was inevitably pulling me in along with Vlad, and the situation was not unfamiliar. I used to have a similar thing with Ilya. With Ilya, I felt at all times like I was in a war, and at no point did I really knew whether I was losing or winning, since he usually had a somewhat different kind of war going on.

And what about the time when I could get to Moscow to stay with Ilya? Something seemed irrevocably lost. Would I be able to get back at least a part of my former life?

I instantly brushed those thoughts aside. At this particular time it was important not to lose Vlad; but how? How the hell could I not lose him?! He did not sit still for a minute.

After walking a couple of blocks, I stopped a taxi and asked where I could buy some cranberry and vodka in these parts.

"My boyfriend caught a cold," I explained.

"What about antibiotics?" the driver asked.

"Antibiotics don't really warm you up. He's got a fever, so I'd better get something to heat up his insides."

"With that Finnish logic of yours I would never come out of a soak, over here," the driver said.

With that horrible Deutsch of mine, I seemed Finnish to him. The driver was Middle Eastern in appearance and he probably caught colds in this country quite often. He made a call to a female friend of his and quickly took me to her house, then in a couple of minutes he turned up with cranberry and a bottle of vodka, and drove me back home.

Vlad was asleep. Those sleepless nights had exhausted him. I hardly touched his shoulder but Vlad startled and instantly opened his eyes. I gave him some vodka and cranberry crushed in sugar.

"Is it Finnish vodka?" he grumbled.

"Yes, they make it especially for the kind of deer like you, with cranberry. You'll be back on your feet tomorrow."

"Hmm... the bitter taste of Moscow... Give me some more."

After he'd had a proper drink and changed his T-shirt, Vlad instantly dozed off.

I could not sleep. I paced up and down the kitchen with a lit cigarette. I recollected Victor. When staying in a small house in Magdeburg with me, he'd said, *This is a trap, but not quite for me...*

What if this trap was not for Harvey Smith but for Vlad Holt?

In fact, there was an obvious reason to eliminate Vlad: it was the deal itself. Someone had tried to seize the arrangement as a whole and had probably spent quite a few years collecting blackmail material to knock out the bank and Vlad at the same time. But who could have discovered that Vlad Holt and sleeper Harvey Smith were one and the same person? That party had known about Vlad since long ago and was probably close to intelligence circles, yet had nothing to do with what had actually happened to Vlad. All they wanted was the deal - that is, without Vlad.

Vlad thought the British Intelligence probably had a reason to burn him up. It appeared the defector, who had settled in London, actually knew he was Harvey Smith; yet he was unaware of him being also Vlad Holt.

And as weird as it looked, Vlad felt that the invader had been informed of Vlad's prospective arrest, but was not mixed up in it. What was all this nonsense?

CHAPTER TWELVE

TRUST ME

I walked out up to the pay phone and dialed the number. Oh God, I could hear Victor's voice. He told me just a few words: *In London, there is no one. He's a banker, Schumann.* Victor almost spelled it out, as if he knew I would hear this message. He left no telephone number and said he would call back soon.

Oh my goodness! And we had thought, all this time, that the Russian defector whom the British intended to cover was staying in London. We could not have been mistaken. The whole patchwork seemed to fall into a beautiful pattern of death. What could it mean?

Upon my return I scanned the news. It was rather risky to log on the Internet, so Vlad purchased a collection of media on a few discs. We did not really need anything beyond that.

The banker Martin Schumann was no big shot. He was a graduate of Stanton University who later returned to Germany. He owned a minor bank so that all his funds could fit into his single pocket.

This bank was identified in a case of money laundering, and alongside him there were also listed Deutsche Bank, Dresdner Bank, and Kommerzbank. Surely none of these banks was directly processing any illegal transactions, but their bank accounts could have been used to transfer the money of a Russian who exported defense equipment. They said the analysis of the money flow in these accounts could help the investigation on BoNY. This kind of assistance was requested by a minor bank. They had to either replace the leader of that bank or obtain his consent by means of this kind of shakedown. The bank manager was expected in court. He had been given notice of the money laundry charges. And the charge of espionage was a cherry on top.

I had to awaken Vlad.

"Vlad, this is the banker." I quickly briefed him on what they wanted to get from him. "Victor told me there is no one in London. Then why the hell is this British Intelligence? Whom do they cover, if there is really no one?"

"They are covering the banker, silly," Vlad uttered in a low voice, trying to return to sleep.

"But why?!"

"I'd like to ask them that question myself, mein herz."

With a lungful of icy air, after a drink of vodka I slept like a log. In the morning I had no desire to get up. The room turned chilly and the sun was hardly shining through the dim, foggy windows. The house smelled of coffee and cologne. Vlad was already on his feet. He was well-shaved. Shit.

"Where are you going?" I asked him.

"I've got to go, now. Your coffee is getting cold."

"Vlad, were you acquainted with that banker?" I inquired, grudgingly throwing off my blanket.

"No. I can't remember him … Look, I've overlooked something important," Vlad said. "I thought this banker was the same as me; a useless, sleeping agent with his only fault being that of taking a too big a piece of the cake. But I'm American and he is German. In the US, they may charge you with espionage even after fifty years; there is no limitation period whatsoever. But in Germany, there is a reasonable time after which no charges of espionage can be filed just because whatever the man in question could have known before is considered hopelessly outdated, so it makes no sense. Oh, shit. I feel myself to be a walking rarity," Vlad cut himself short.

"So what?"

"That's in case they bring charges against the banker on this side. It would mean he is an active agent," Vlad explained. "And the game is totally different for an active agent. If they got a witness to confirm the same, I would be of no use to him in this situation, even from that coffin of mine. Now it seems clear why he cannot be charged of tax evasion."

"The banker's found you by himself. And that dead defector may have known him."

"Yes, the British need a bad source like me to drag the Americans into this case and present the banker as a long-forgotten sleeper, not an active agent. I can't really tell."

"Vlad, you should move away. I'm begging you."

"I've got an idea. It may work out. I can't be Harvey Smith, neither dead nor alive. Could this all turn out to be totally different from what it seems to be now? Could they just need that Vlad Holt? Maybe I have underestimated the invader?"

"What's on your mind?"

"That'll work fine, don't you worry," Vlad said in contemplation. "I'll go to the embassy and sign my confessionary statement, and if it all works out the way I'm thinking now, everything will be fine. In a word, if they got a really good lawyer, then ... that might be not so easy, but I don't give a fuck anymore. Don't you worry about me."

While Vlad was telling me this, I could not believe my ears, and a wave of rage and annoyance covered my face. I could feel it burning,

"Vlad, what are you talking about? Do you want to draw up your confession? Have you gone mad?"

"And what is your suggestion? Should I keep still till they get me packed into a coffin and bring me to court? My lawyer is waiting for me. Early in the morning, I went out to make a call to him. By the way, you sleep like... One could easily carry you away feet first and you would not wake up. Well, trust me."

I could seize him by his sleeve or jump down his throat, but that would not really help. Vlad was making decisions on his own. I believe he actually knew more than me. Having been in all kinds of situations, he was able to foresee more than I could ever guess. I had to trust his gut feeling. I was totally at sea as to what was happening, so what could I tell him? I could not really stop him.

CHAPTER THIRTEEN

THE FINAL FLOURISH

Four hours later I went out into the street. The chilly wind of humid air was burning my face, and without thinking much about anything, I entered a pastry shop, drank a cup of coffee, and asked for a mini-cake. On my way out I bumped into Vlad.

"Vlad, what are you doing here? What the deuce are you doing walking in here under the cams?!"

"I've written my statement. It's all over," Vlad answered.

Vlad told me he'd paid a visit to the US embassy. He called himself Harvey Smith and told them everything: that he had noticed the surveillance and thought he was going to be kidnapped and taken to Moscow, so he decided to come forward with a confessionary statement. They were not ready for his visit. They kept Vlad waiting for an hour, and then he was offered to sign a statement where they gave him the name of the banker he had to mention as the agent who was recruited at the same time as he. In exchange, they agreed not to bring charges of high treason against him. These were mere words.

Two hours after signing the statement, Vlad's lawyer turned up before the judge to explain that even with the handwriting expert and Vlad's signature, any linguistic expert would be able to prove that this was not his own style and that this confession was taken at someone's dictation, and he had not really known the banker in question. The man who had received Vlad at the embassy had dictated these sentences to him without much thought. That trick would not have worked the presence of a qualified lawyer. And if Vlad had lingered somewhat, the embassy would have been ready for his visit.

Even if that trick of his had not worked, Vlad would have risked signing that statement anyway, as he could see no other way out.

The judge confirmed that he would not accept the confession. And if the judge or anyone else there ever asked why Andreas Leman decided to claim he was the former agent Harvey Smith, Vlad could tell them he had been offered the job for a few thousand dollars. That is why the jury never believed in conversations recorded by FBI dummies. What person would not tell you of themselves for a hundred dollars, even about them being a Russian agent?

That actually meant this confession was nothing but a slip of paper, and Vlad was common German citizen Andreas Leman unless they could prove he was someone else. But on this side of the pond, they would prefer to brush it under the carpet.

They could no longer use Vlad as a former agent for a cover-up. And if somebody still wanted to do so, Vlad was no longer presentable in court. And if they retrieved his files and he was again seen as a former agent, that would only mean a mild term in a US prison. One way or another, Vlad could no longer serve for this action, even as a dead witness.

Vlad said that deep down inside, he actually wanted to return, and when making his way to the embassy, he'd thought this outcome was still possible ... become Harvey Smith again and start everything from scratch...

Two blocks from our accommodations, we separated and went in different directions. Vlad made his way home and I headed to the hotel where I usually turned up towards evening and went out again in bright makeup, as if I was going to tour the late-night bars.

I'd hardly stepped into the hotel lobby when the receptionist stopped me and said in a soft low voice,

"I'm so sorry, Frau Holt, but your husband has died. Please accept my condolences."

She wanted to say it again, but I stopped her with a gesture. It was all clear. I was at loss and I felt nauseated. Vlad just made two steps forward and then turned around to take the carton of mini-cakes from my hands.

His face looked as if it were parboiled with frost, his eyebrows and lashes as white as if the snow had never melted from his face. He seemed so alive. I was still watching him leave, in his hat pulled over his forehead and his crooked shoulders under a coat soiled by wear. He looked different; so plain and third-rate - and then after another few steps I lost sight of him.

The things we had been discussing and everything else resembled a delirious dream. I felt I was out of touch with reality. If only I had known... I should have listened to Vlad, and understood what was really happening. No, I should have convinced him to escape as far as he could and flee as soon as possible. How could I have just observed him waiting for his death? I failed to believe him. It had all gone over so very fast and it was all so complicated and unintelligible.

I had seen no threat. How could I have noticed it if nothing was really happening? And I'd had no gut feelings, either. Yes, Vlad had been waiting for his arrest; but he should have been arrested right away, two weeks earlier. This had largely disconcerted us. Vlad had waited for god knows what. And we'd had nothing but his suppositions, and just kept on speaking and drinking vodka. How could we have missed such a drastic change of the situation there was now no way back?

Someone had already planned everything that was to happen to Vlad. Why, fully aware of this, would Vlad still be reflecting about things? Why did not he just escape? How was it possible? He'd been aware of something else that he was unable to explain to me. How could one clarify his whole life in just two or three days? Why had I failed to sense that something was going on? Why this stupor?

The receptionist slipped a slip of paper into my hand with the telephone number left by the police officer. I walked out into the street.

Death can be sensed from afar... Now, hold on. This was no death but some other kind of shit. There seemed to be no logic in it - it just could not be true. I went back to the hotel to inquire about the time of the police officer's visit. It turned out he'd dropped in just one hour before. And one hour earlier, I had been buying my mini cake. So what could have happened? To find me here would have also taken some time; so this was not Vlad. But, who?!

Oh Lord, could it be someone else, not Vlad? Oh Lord, could you do something? Don't you sit still - oh my God, could you please do something?!

Growing cold in the chilly wind with its snow haze, feeling impotent rage, I was thinking: *I know you died here, my Lord. This is why it is so easy for me to live here under these skies.*

I was almost running. I could see Vlad's footprints on the pathway and on the porch against the recent snow. His footprints! I flew up the stairs to breathe in the fragrance of cigarettes mixed with the cold humid air. There was nothing better, to me, than this smell. I opened the door into the smoky rooms and saw Vlad's silhouette. He was hunching his crooked shoulders over the paperwork, just like through all these other days and nights. His spectacles glistened from the screen light.

Oh, I was so happy to see him again!

"Vlad!! I was told you were dead! I was identified as your wife by the police, and they notified of your death! Who died? Oh God, you are alive! I can't believe my eyes, now!"

Vlad looked at me perplexedly for a split second,

"Oh my goodness, I'm so very glad to hear this," he sighed in relief, and stood up.

"What does it mean, your badass mother?!"

"Hmm..." Vlad pulled me in and hugged me. "That actually means I can live. That is the main thing. I've got no idea what else this could mean. Fuck if I know this British classic. Nothing can change it. And here you understand that a perfect lawn is something that's been groomed for three hundred years. Oh, I feel so fucked up here, just like after some heavy porn. And you?"

"Vodka?"

"Yes. With cranberry. I prefer not to think about anything now. Damn it all. Would you like a cake?"

Like this book?

Maybe you leave a review?

WHO SPREADS FOR WHOM
Book Two of The Sleeper Series

by Anna Schlegel

ISBN: 9780998185385
ASIN: B06WLGZ444

The British Intelligence cannot compromise its integrity; it will adhere to its principles like in the old times of rock 'n roll. And it's damn good to see it working... but then, it's scary to see it work against you.

They seemed to be looking for a perfect witness for that legal action. One was a sleeper, another a dead sleeper, and the third was a dummy agent. While this man alone passed for all three, he was never summoned to court.

You may wish to learn a bit more about the legendary agent, and these books would most likely catch your eye. Will you be able to find within them the answer to the question of whether Philby was indeed a legendary spy? I doubt it.

A Spy Among Friends: Kim Philby and the Great Betrayal
by Ben Macintyre, John le Carré

To my mind, it's a better idea to read Phillip Knightley. He starts his book from the point when he stepped across the threshold of Kim Philby's apartment in Moscow. This book has an answer.

Philby: KGB Mastermind
by Phillip Knightley

I'm writing about Kim Philby from a different side; that is, from the side where he used to be loved, and where he remains as a living legend.

From Russia with love,

Anna Schlegel

THE GODS SMILE ON THE BASTARDS

Book Three of The Sleeper Series

by Anna Schlegel

ISBN: 9780998185392
ASIN: B06XYVGTK6

Once you are able to see intelligence's hand, you may see the words of failure inscribed in the same handwriting - a failure they are yet unaware of

By looking at that other man from afar, he found it hard to shake off the feeling of looking at his own self from the outside. That other man resembled him way too much. The man was better than him, more experienced and farfetched, and he looked more convincing, and rather a slime ball. Everyone could see it. The man succeeded in making everyone around believe he was truly him, in person. And the man could prove it. What would eventually happen if the man slipped off? Then the only guy remaining there would be himself. And he would be constrained to be more like his former self. For all those long years, he had plain forgotten what kind of person he was underneath. He would have to recollect this and become somewhat more life-like. He would hardly be able to make it, really, unless he was dead. But then, would it be a preferable option - something they truly wanted?

Why do intelligence people become turncoats? There may be two answers. One is obvious. They become turncoats due to a landmark case against other turncoats. Every agent, while keeping a close watch on the case, usually dissects the defendant's mistakes, so he thinks he would never do anything similar; that he could do things smarter, with a lot more caution...

The second answer is something else. People come to be turncoats long before they start working for the spy directorate. So read it all: this is worth knowing. This is the answer from a legend. Listen to it, give it a touch, and you'll be blessed with a smile of God.

ONLY ONE REALITY THAT KILLS

Book Four of The Sleeper Series

by Anna Schlegel

ISBN: 9780999127605

It happens to everyone without exception. It will inevitably happen to you unless you live under the wing of the legend.

He was back. No one believed it was him until he started killing those who had no more doubts.

LIE MAKES ME LIVE
Book Five of The Sleeper Series

by Anna Schlegel

Coming soon

This game of the intelligence, we were either to see through it, or die.

There is an old brain teaser about three different gods, God of Lie, God of Truth and God of Chance. One of them lied all the time, another told everyone the truth only, and the third one could either tell the truth or lie. So who of them was who in there?

Who was that man? There happened to be three people who had told they knew the man. So who of them could be telling the truth? And who must have been lying? Who could have been led up the path? And what kind of person was he himself? He was the only man to know the answer, but he was the God of Lie.

ABOUT THE AUTHOR

Why do I know so much of the Intelligence? It must have come from between the bedsheets, and not just this much. Victor returned to Moscow after a few years of work as a financial expert. He was more of a moneyman than a special service agent, even more he was a swindler. He became a raider like so many others, during those years. He used to have both good luck and failure in bank seizures, in which he lost money. I imperceptibly turned to be just the same like him.

These books are written from an adventurer's perspective. There are no good guys, since those good guys have no chance of attracting a female. Women want bastards.

Why read my books? I've got the undeniable strength of being a Russian author, which means that I'm writing about the Russian Intelligence without using much fiction.

Of course, these are just mere fiction novels, a kind of multi-twist mind game; yet I'm describing events the way they could have touched me in reality. So these books actually represent my "might-have-been" by seizing the fact that I could have lived a number of alternative lives. Understandably, one life is enough for me: my behind would hardly stand more adventures. I'm writing about things that I find interesting. I've only read a few books of spy fiction - for the most part, they are deadly boring.

I was born in Moscow. I studied at the Moscow State University at the Philosophical facility. I got a PhD in philosophy and stayed without work and without money. The financial crisis began. Some years I looked for a work, but took it easy. I became a securities trader in an investment company by chance. And then came the default in 1998. I was without work again.

This was my best time. I became the financial middleman for off-market private transactions. I had nothing. I had been looking for too-big deals. But then there was a time when it was quite possible for me to be the middleman in the sale of a Libyan oil tanker or for the sale of an aircraft abroad. I got sick of conducting multi-million dollar transactions and lost all sense of reality.

I met Victor. Capturing the bank was in my sights. The insider of the bank was its vice-president. I write about his capture almost verbatim. Before leaving, he gave me his three passports... So I do not know his real name. There were no closed doors for him. He had friends from the federal agency for government communication and information from the board of directors of Deutsche Bank. All kinds of people.

Years passed. Victor is long gone. And there are fewer middlemen.

I feel myself to be on the way out. My whole generation is on the way out as well; those who are described as robbing the country.

I like those who robbed the country, and I'm pleased about how it was done. They were really talented financiers; nothing worse than the financiers on Wall Street. They left the country and took the money with them.

Since then, Moscow's air did not smell of millions any longer. But, it seemed to me, it was still in the depths of my house between a pile of white shirts. Now there are no more financial middlemen. The young have gotten jobs first. They receive a salary at the end of the month, and seem to have already forgotten the smell of crazy millions. It's like being drunk. There's a dizziness from it ... They did not want to breathe this air. They did not want to poison their lives. They earned their money. They had wives, children, dogs, and cars, which it was necessary to care of... Their heads have overflowed with thoughts of petty cash.

Then the middlemen were old. And I stayed with them. Therefore, the heroes of my novels are in their sixties. To the former friends who stayed in the stock market, I became infected. No, I just died. And I smell of sweet cadaveric decay. It seemed to me that I was among the dead. And it felt really bad for me, as a living being. But I shared their way of thinking. I was the same as they were: ridiculous and old-fashioned, useless clutter, rubbish. Market garbage. My friends were precisely the same as middle-aged gentlemen.

Sometimes I catch a strange look directed towards me, but then forget about it. The metropolis wiped me from their memory. There was no need to be as nice as kind people who talk with clients and colleagues daily. I had a different way of talking. My talking always led to a deal. And if it didn't, I would give the finger and immediately forget the useless person, as if shaking off dust. And that's all.

I have nothing to regret. I had nothing to blame

myself for. Dogs wouldn't blame themselves for their dog's life, would they?

I cannot return to the stock market. It has changed. Brokers, buyers, and sellers have been changed. They all grew up a little. They have got each other for 0.1 percent interest, ready to sell their ass to everyone at 0.5 percent, and would sell their own mother at one percent. I could not do that. The market has kicked me out as garbage.

And the old, among whom I used to be, are gone. The reality of small money has burned out people all around me as fire burns wood. Sometimes it seems to me that I have gone mad; that I live in a world turned inside out. Sometimes I would like to be like anyone... to have a rest, eat, dress, buy a car...

But I can't do it. It would be a living death.

It seems to me I would lose days and years and would end up in devastation and poverty. And I would lose the scent of money, and my skills ... so I clung to the sale of oil, diamonds, and bank guarantees, though I'm sure that it was simply thin air and there was nothing behind it. Sometimes I woke up and thought that all was not with me. But I lived and breathed the air of millions. It was my life. In my life, I gained money from thin air. Emptiness is a magnet for me.

Now I have got nothing. I do not care. I like my life. I like to go for millions. It's impossible to stop me. I might have to be put down like a mad dog.

And I still have a sense of money. I can smell the street's air and say that the market has changed. It smells as sharp as the smell of fresh bread from a bakery in the winter.

THE DEAD BANK DIARY SERIES

THE DEAD BANK DIARY
Book One of The Dead Bank Diary Series
ISBN: 9780986174919
ASIN: B00OPAZQMI

FOR THOSE IN THE SHADE
Book Two of The Dead Bank Diary Series
ISBN: 9780986174964
ASIN: B014Q92DE6

THE PRINTS ON THE SNOWS OF YESTERYEAR
Book Three of The Dead Bank Diary Series
ISBN: 9780986174988
ASIN: B017KYY2MA

SOME DAY I'LL HIT A BANK
Book Four of The Dead Bank Diary Series
ISBN: 9780998185323
ASIN: B01LYZ3XQX

THE FROZEN DEBT
Book Five of The Dead Bank Diary Series
ISBN: 9780998185309
ASIN: B01LX1AKZ7

AUTHOR'S NOTE

In these books there are no cops; no killings. There is much about the illegal takeover of banks, and a powerful amount of money. I know how to pump up a bank, and how to bankrupt one. I love beautiful gray schemes on the verge of being crimes. My stories are about fraud as seen through the eyes of a swindler. There are no good guys.

I write about the golden-time bankers from 1998, when neither the police nor the intelligence services, or any crimes, prevented the banks from making money.

These novels are not based on a true story, but you will face this reality in every word.

ABOUT THE DEAD BANK DIARY SERIES

These are stories about a man who is not alive anymore. He was a financier; a retired intelligence officer. I had the good luck to arrange a couple of financial frauds. We bumped into each other before the recession, in the flood of shit, and were together in the dust.

After his death, I still had the power of attorney.

Of course, Victor knew I wouldn't be able to work his contacts. I had tried. Now it's funny to think of it. I am, and have always been, a go-between; a rat. Nobody needs middlemen. They get rid of them; they send them to Hell. But I had a white shirt with a necktie and copies of million dollar contracts for oil, gas, diamonds, and rare-earth metals: light as air, rolled fax sheets with lots of zeroes. They made me giddy; they made me drunk. And I ran along with them, and easily foisted them onto the middlemen: muddy, middle-aged misters.

When some of the first deals failed, I went into hysterics. I wanted to throw in the towel.

Once I had a dream. In my dream, I listened to a telephone call: "Miss Schlegel? We need your signature to extend a contract concluded by Mr..."

I woke up scared; something turned over inside of me. I realized that I was spending my life waiting for such a call. It didn't matter where it caught me.

But there was no going back. Once you've taken a step forward, you realize you can't turn back anymore.

Why did he leave all this to me? I looked over the papers, recalling past years, deals, people, talks - everything from the first meeting to the last minute. And I couldn't find anything for me; because it wasn't for me, actually, but for the old me. So I changed. I became a con.

My life was changed. Sometimes it was as convincing and disgusting as the life of a whore. It was as inaccessible as the man who despises you. It was like vomit or sweat from the body from a heavy hangover's shivers. You wish to run, but there's no place to run to. It's a cold stupor. So it's stupid to look at the smeared corpse on the road, and it's impossible to regain consciousness to look away. This passion nests in the heart, and you don't know what it is.

I have his photo, the last one, taken at Arkhangelskoe hospital. Summer. We're sitting on the edge of a dried-up fountain. He embraces me with one arm, and I'm lost next to him. He is gray-haired and corpulent. He has a mocking look. And behind us there are towering white marble angels.

THE DEAD BANK DIARY

Book One of The Dead Bank Diary Series

by Anna Schlegel

ISBN: 9780986174919
ASIN: B00OPAZQMI

---

*The rats living on the refuse of the bank's backyard stay full
at all times*

This is not a robbery. A bank is taken with all its guts: accounts, debts, points of exchange, the staff down to the last secretary, the building. This is beautiful and clean fraud.

I was out of work, while all around, you could smell millions even in the air outside. It was an unforgettable smell of public debt, oilfields, gold, bank guarantees, diamonds... I wanted to breathe in the air of easy cash Moscow, to revel and roll in this air. I could feel the smell of money in the wind on my face. This air was used to make up funds overnight; to make a fortune, go to rack and ruin, and then grow rich again. It was blowing freely across the wreckage of the sold-out Soviet empire.

I was asked to help redeem the debts of a bank. The insider man at the bank held the post of Vice President.

A bit of danger and a bit of love.

FOR THOSE IN THE SHADE

Book Two of The Dead Bank Diary Series

by Anna Schlegel

ISBN: 9780986174964
ASIN: B014Q92DE6

You may live your whole life without getting to know who you are, and sometimes this is for the better

It was a bank robbery. However, this time the gunmen came not for the cash but for the bank itself, and all that followed happened faster than a domino knockdown.

The bank was bankrupted professionally.

Bad debts of the Third World countries, Cuba, Zimbabwe, Morocco, and The Congo, have been returned to the bank's balance sheet. Once, the bank sold the debts to itself; to an offshore company.

Who did this?

The banker finds the bank in Amsterdam... and has taken it over completely.

THE PRINTS ON THE SNOWS OF YESTERYEAR

Book Three **of** The Dead Bank Diary Series

by Anna Schlegel

ISBN: 9780986174988
ASIN: B017KYY2MA

The best one to rob the bank is the banker himself

The bank, facing bankruptcy, fell out of his hands like a snowball rolling downhill to flatten everything under its weight.

Behind every bankruptcy, there are people who make it happen. But there are no influential people. Big figures are absent. It seems you stay face to face with the emptiness.

This happens when the Central Bank is playing against you.

SOME DAY I'LL HIT A BANK

Book Four of The Dead Bank Diary Series

by Anna Schlegel

ISBN: 9780998185323
ASIN: B01LYZ3XQX

The bomb lives to its internal time

My life became lonely and monotonous, almost mechanical in nature, with a mechanism akin to a ticking bomb. It could be ticking for days and weeks, quiet and imperceptible, only to blow up everything around at the right time.

This is the way common folks used to live in the past; bakers and shoemakers. They lived their lives until the revolution burst out. It was their time. And then they went out the door of their bakery and shoe shop for good, to take the ministry chairs and cut the heads off the aristocracy by weaving plots and intrigues. I knew I would not miss my time.

It seemed to me I could go on for another ten years, only to one day stumble on a terse line in the newspaper and realize: my time has come.

THE FROZEN DEBT

Book Five of The Dead Bank Diary Series

by Anna Schlegel

ISBN: 9780998185309
ASIN: B01LX1AKZ7

When the totally nude have a look, maybe you still have the shoulder loops

One morning he stayed bare-ass. There was no money, no name, no wife, and nothing left... just his shoulder loops.

The deal Victor had set up six years ago kept running like clockwork and suddenly came to a halt. The accounts of the company formerly owned by Victor were blocked by the public prosecution. The man who found Victor in Moscow offered to give him everything back: his company and his board membership and ... his wife.

Upon his arrival in Berlin, Victor realized that all parties wanted a goner.

And Victor was an ideal goner, as he was also a mole.

Anna Schlegel has a degree in philosophy. She was a securities trader before the recession. For the last ten years she has been involved in off-market private transactions as a middleman in Moscow.

Anna lives in Novi Sad, Serbia.

CONTACTS INFORMATION

For information about the author, please visit TheSleeper.club

thedeadbankdiary@gmail.com

For information about the published books, please contact Schlegel Press Association at

schlegelpressassociation@gmail.com